Thieves, Beasts & Men

A NOVEL

SHAN LEAH

Arcade Publishing • New York

First Arcade Edition

Arcade Publishing books may be purchased in bulk at special discounts for sales promotion, corporate gifts, fund-raising, or educational purposes. Special editions can also be created to specifications. For details, contact the Special Sales Department, Arcade Publishing, 307 West 36th Street, 11th Floor, New York, NY 10018 or arcade@skyhorsepublishing.com.

Arcade Publishing® is a registered trademark of Skyhorse Publishing, Inc.®, a Delaware corporation.

Visit our website at www.arcadepub.com.

10 9 8 7 6 5 4 3 2 1

Library of Congress Cataloging-in-Publication Data is available on file.

Cover design by Erin Seaward-Hiatt
Cover artwork: Shan Leah

ISBN: 978-1-951627-97-3
Ebook ISBN: 978-1-950994-08-3

Printed in the United States of America

DEDICATION

For my grandmother Diane, who wrote books in the last years of her life but passed away before she saw them published. I *began* this book for you.

For my grandmother Patricia, who inspired a love of words, and read the first parts of my manuscript before she passed away. I *finished* this book for you.

❁

A girl who has never spoken a word chirps a sound into the forest.

Flies land on her cheek, and she reaches into the mud, smearing it across her face to keep the bugs away. Mother taught her that.

The girl is hungry, and an unfamiliar smell leads her to a place that looks like a small, square forest inside the forest. She crawls along the ground, sniffing everything—big, round things the color of the sun, and long things that smell like water plants, and heavy things with peeling skin that make tears drip from her eyes.

The girl sits up on her knees and chirps again, putting a hand to her ear so she can hear better. Mother taught her that, too.

There is no response.

Something catches her eye, and the girl crawls across the square forest and holds it in her hands. It is soft and round, and the color of the bird that makes the *yeep* sound. She pushes into it with her finger and warm, sticky juice runs down her arm. The girl licks it. She can't wait to show mother and brother what she has found.

The girl gathers as many things from this strange place as she can carry, and leaves the small, square forest inside the forest. She barks a stunted syllable into the trees, and someone barks back. The girl grins, bouncing on her knees. She takes a big bite of the soft, round thing with the warm, sticky juice, and then disappears into the forest.

❁

PART 1
THIEVES

1

Adelaide arranges the pills on the window ledge and counts them as they wobble. The prescription label warns, "No more than 2 pills within a 24-hour period," and "Contact Poison Control Center immediately," in red. But the pills are very old and surely not as potent as they once were, so she counts out more, and drops ten pills into her pocket.

Adelaide catches her reflection in the small, round mirror by the front door, grimacing at the woman who stares back. She's an old lady now—it happened after all. Adelaide touches the landscape of her forehead, those lines like a natural disaster. My god, how she's earned this.

She massages her joints with shaky fingers and glances one last time at her empty cabin, before walking out the door. She does not lock it.

Adelaide dreads another winter. Hers is a farmer's life, its lessons buried in her flesh like veins of garnet. When an animal is suffering, a swift, painless death is a kindness. Humans are no different.

She has made her decision.

The first pill lodges in her throat, and Adelaide feels it like a river stone. The second pill pushes it down into her gut.

The bitter wind lashes her face—it seems the seasons turn faster and faster every year.

The fifth pill goes down as smoothly as the third and the fourth. Five little pills dissolving in her belly. Five little reasons to keep walking.

There is a place Adelaide wishes to be today, on her last day—her secret spot, where the water catches on the rocks and forms a symphonic eddy beneath the maple tree. It is a short trek up the riverside, but now, at the end of autumn, the fallen leaves coat the ground like a plush carpet, ushering Adelaide forward. It is just up ahead. She hears it now, the sound of spinning currents, as another pill disappears down her throat.

By the time Adelaide reaches the eddy, she has empty pockets, and her head already swims. She removes her clothes, item by item, folds them into neat squares beside the tree, and sits. The leaves have reddened and dropped, and they pool at her feet. She gathers the ruby leaves, placing them in her hair. Nestled in the taut strands of her bun, an auburn crown.

Adelaide's vision darkens and flutters, and the river suddenly shrinks from view. Her lungs are a pair of masonry bricks lodged in her chest, as dense with concrete as with oxygen. Her tongue is fuzzy and sticks to the roof of her mouth. She peels it off like a bandage.

It's happening too fast.

Adelaide longs to feel the cold river on her cheek one last time. She tries to drag herself to the water's edge, into its swells of cream and gray, but her body is rigid and numb. She wants the water to coat her like paint, hardening and tightening around her. She wants it to soak her silver hair black as she disappears beneath the surface. But first, she must move her legs before it's too late.

Adelaide pulls herself to her knees, refusing to die right here, under the maple tree. The water surges against the riverbed, splashing her face. She can feel it, taste it.

But her body is too heavy, and she sinks to the ground, the river a thousand miles away. Adelaide curses herself for her weakness, slamming her limp wrists against the earth.

Sprawled on the bank, her breathing begins to slow, and Adelaide is mere feet from the water's edge when everything goes black.

The lantern is still lit. How careless; she knows better.

Adelaide stumbles into the kitchen and grips the edge of the sink.

Mud sheets from her clothes, leaving a winding puddle across her floor. She coughs, and liquid froths from her lungs, painting her tongue. It is gritty and sour; she swallows it down.

Adelaide closes her eyes and tries to remember how long she was at the river, and how she got home. The harder she searches her mind for memories of her journey back, the hazier they become, until she questions her recollection of disrobing at all. She pulls a red leaf from her tangled hair and flings it into the sink.

Night falls quickly in the Blue Ridge Mountains, and the forest is already changing to shades of slate and plum. Her reflection in the window stares back at her, the wetness sparkling off every fleshy fold, as if age is something to swathe in glitter. She pulls a hand down her face and watches the skin draw toward her chin.

All she'd wanted was a death of her own choosing, her own making. Her last act in this world, and she has failed. Adelaide sighs, too tired to think any longer, and she walks to her bedroom. Tomorrow, she will try again. Tomorrow, she will take *twenty* pills.

Morning light surges through her window as if this day were any other. Zelda and Moffit scratch outside her bedroom window, upending today's offering of beetles and larva. She hears their gentle clucks, their lilting conversation—whatever it is that chickens discuss in the early morning. Adelaide waits. It'll happen any minute now; he's never far behind the girls. Ah yes—there he is. Henry crows his raspy lament to the rising sun. Such a pitiful sound—he never quite mastered the majesty of a proper cock-a-doodle-do.

Adelaide watches the stains on her ceiling slowly come into focus before forcing herself to sit. Stand. Yesterday's clothes sag from her body, plaited around her torso. The fabric is discolored from wet leaves and soil, as is her skin, and the river tempts her with one final bath. Adelaide stumbles across her cabin, her mind thick with disorientation. The pills must still be lingering in her system. So be it—less chance of failure today.

She disrobes and steps into the morning air, staggering down the narrow path by her cabin. On even the brightest of days, the canopies in the forest are dense, their shadows a black smudge on an otherwise brilliant canvas.

Adelaide no longer covers her nakedness as she nears the river—it's been years since she's seen a stranger so deep in the mountains. Besides, who is she to deny a wayward hiker a small thrill?

As Adelaide settles into the river, the water grips her with cold, despite the sun filtering through the canopy like shimmering flakes of gold leaf.

Adelaide grasps handfuls of clay and sand, buffing the earth into her calves, her shins, her elbows and shoulders, between her toes. She scrubs until she feels that pleasant rawness, that freshly birthed pink on her flesh.

Adelaide stays in the water longer than usual. She should have fed the chickens by now. On a normal day, she would tend to the garden, gather wood, or can last week's overabundance of vegetables. Anything other than lounge in the river. But today is not a normal day.

Today, Adelaide does not have to prepare for another winter.

Today, on her last day, she can be lazy.

She watches two snakes twist and twine on the riverside. To the untrained eye, it would seem as though they are locked in battle. The smaller snake moves as though injured, bending and contorting into angles that could only mean death. But Adelaide knows better. Somewhere within the mass of black and oily skin, they are joined. The snakes break free and slip soundlessly into the water. They are the poisonous kind—Adelaide knows this—but she does not care to move right now.

She burrows her toes into the silt, and another mushroom cloud of gray earth blooms at her feet.

Today, Adelaide will dress in white.

She put little thought into pageantry the day before, but now she thinks that wearing white has some level of poetry to it.

Adelaide decides on a long white skirt and an old white sweater she knitted for herself more than a decade earlier. She shakes it out and dust fills the bedroom. It is stained, ill-fitting, and the moth holes are larger than she remembers. It is perfect. She slips it over her head, the wool like a receiving blanket swaddled around her shoulders.

The walk to the kitchen is practiced and automatic, as if the routine were engraved on her skin. Hips go left to avoid the corner stool, footsteps wide to dodge that one floorboard that pulls away from the nails.

The pill bottle is on the counter, right where she left it. She hopes there are enough, but she doesn't reach for the bottle. Not yet. Adelaide strikes a match and a small flame ignites before her fingertips, bathing them in a warm, honey glaze. As the flame dwindles, a ribbon of smoke pirouettes before her like a dancer, and she steps into the living room and lights the lantern.

Adelaide fetches the amber pill bottle and holds it against the glow. The little white discs tumble into her little pale hand, and she tucks them into the pocket of her long white skirt.

Outside the window, Henry struts across the grass, leading Zelda and Moffit toward the thicket behind her cabin. Adelaide misses fresh eggs, but the girls stopped laying years earlier. Adelaide decided long ago not to eat them, though maybe now. . . . It's been so long since she's hunted or fished. She barely remembers the taste of meat. But Adelaide decides she doesn't want to know what Henry and the girls taste like.

Above the kitchen sink are a dozen sunflowers, cut and hanging. Wilted leaves like rolled tobacco, seeds bulging from each head like swollen ticks. No sense in leaving them here to rot and mold and turn to dust. Adelaide gathers as many flowers as she can hold and rips them from the hooks, raining threads of stalk into the sink.

The pills rattle in her pocket, but they can wait—the chickens deserve one last snack.

Adelaide steps outside her door and into the small clearing between the river path and her garden, squinting into the sunlight.

"Here girls! Here Henry!"

Three feathered bodies emerge from behind her cabin, scampering into view. Henry's feathers are a bit ragged, but he wears his plum neck plume like a jeweled crown. Both Zelda and Moffit are the shade of a newly birthed fawn, their copper feathers smudged with specks of chestnut and black. They are good chickens, and Adelaide hopes they won't miss her too much when she is gone.

Adelaide casts the seeds upon the ground, and Zelda and Moffit devour every one.

Henry ignores the offering and peers up at Adelaide, studying her with his black, pupil-less eyes.

Henry is a devoted protector. Adelaide once watched from a window as he banished a small fox from the henhouse in a storm of talons, beak, and feather. She'd discovered him standing in the garden the following morning, preening himself over a small scrap of bloodied fox fur.

Henry inches toward Adelaide.

"Go on now."

Adelaide waves him away but the rooster comes closer, perching on her feet.

This is not like Henry. His eyes are gentle, but his talons are breaking the skin. She kicks him off and he flutters away in a tantrum of squawks.

Adelaide walks toward her garden, admiring its wattle fence made of willow branches. Once, there was also a gate. As a younger woman,

Adelaide spent two summers weaving the enclosure to deter nosy forest critters. To her surprise, it's been fairly successful.

The garden is more neglected than she had realized. The tomato plants have grown spindly, only a few dented orbs dangling from their limbs. Adelaide could swear there were more tomatoes yesterday. By her feet, one tomato lies covered in dirt. Near to that, a bough has been severed, a small chunk of fruit still attached, wet and pink, seeds spilling like viscera across the soil.

Something has been in her garden.

Adelaide weaves around the beds, examining what is left of the carrot bed, now a massacred mound of soil. Only a few tufts of green have been left behind.

"Oh my . . ."

Adelaide lifts a carrot stalk, and its lanky leaves dangle through her fingers.

Henry and the girls peer into the garden.

"Who did this?" she asks, thrusting the carrot remains toward the three. "Did you do this?"

The chickens stare at her and do not enter. Adelaide knows better. The chickens did not ransack her garden, but she has no one else to scold.

She scans the beds for damage: the cucumbers have dwindled in numbers, the pumpkins are untouched, but the melons have taken casualties, their twisted remnants showered all across the garden. She still has some of her broccoli, but not all. The animal had its fair share of that as well.

Blood pounds at Adelaide's temples. She's never seen destruction like this before. This is not the butchery of a rabbit or groundhog. And no damage has been done to the fence, or even to the leafy mulch Adelaide spread on the paths between the beds. A deer? A small bear, perhaps?

She knows what she needs to do. This is her home, and she will not allow it to be destroyed. She's spent years cultivating this garden—*years!*

Adelaide forces a deep breath and tries to convince herself to let the garden be. Why attempt to keep the scavenger out just to allow the garden to bloom and wilt and turn to seed and rot? *Let 'em have it,* she thinks.

Adelaide looks down. Her white skirt is brown at the bottom. She is no longer fresh and pure. She is no longer pageantry and poetry. Great, that's all an old lady needs right now.

And so Adelaide returns to her cabin and empties her pocket of the pills, returning them to the bottle for safekeeping. Tonight, she will clean her white skirt and knitted sweater, and she will try again tomorrow. The sun is already so high in the sky and there are dirty dishes in the sink that she should wash.

But first . . .

First, she will build a garden gate.

2

Adelaide has spent the afternoon walking to and from the river path, retrieving the largest branches she can carry. Any sane person would tear down the fence, invite the animals in to feast. But a life spent deep in the woods doesn't exactly cultivate sanity, and a little bit of madness has served Adelaide well throughout the years. Far be it from her to stanch it now.

Adelaide stacks the branches side by side upon the ground, tying them together with old bits of fishing line salvaged from her storage shed. She longs for the warmth of the cabin. Her white skirt and sweater are drying by the fireplace, waiting for her, eager for the bottom of the river. Tomorrow. Yes, tomorrow.

Adelaide props the new gate against the wattle fence, securing it as best she can with the fishing line, and steps back to examine her handiwork. The branches are wobbly and don't quite fit the opening, but they should hold.

Henry and the girls toddle toward her, pausing to admire her work. Zelda and Moffit peck around the gate, eager for any bugs that may have been disturbed.

A large, somber cloud, dense as a forest canopy, blocks the sun, cloaking Adelaide in shadow. Adelaide knows these clouds. Now that she's paying attention, she can smell it in the air. How did she not notice earlier? Tonight, a storm is coming.

Adelaide cannot sleep. Perhaps it is the wind, or her rattling windows. Perhaps it is the pill bottle, beckoning from the shadows of the kitchen. She listens for evidence of her garden marauder pouncing on the last of her cantaloupes, but hears nothing through the whistling cyclone.

At times like these, the outside noise creates such a clamor that inner voices and memories surge forward, begging to be noticed. Faces of people she once knew, words spoken but never forgotten, time spent and wasted. But tonight, she thinks of something lovely. Beneath the floorboard in the living room—the one that pulls away from the nails—is a box. It is a box she usually tries to forget, and she doesn't step on the board for fear of remembering, as the elicited emotions are hard to predict and impossible to prepare for. It's a bit like a minefield and she never knows which step will detonate. But tonight, she summons the memory with ease, and there are no bombs.

Once, many years ago, there was a tall mirror by her bedroom door, and the wind through the open windows would rattle the frame against the wall. She sees herself, young, hair long and thickened by the hormones coursing through her veins. Standing before the mirror and parting the buttons of her dress until it falls from her shoulders, dangling from her hips. Watching her body in the reflection, as though she can witness its minute changes if only she can find the right angle. Running her hands over her growing womb and pressing on her navel, which had recently begun to bulge. Wrapping her arms around her belly, no longer alone.

Adelaide sits up and brings her stiff hands to her face. It seems as though tonight she has, in fact, detonated a bomb.

The tears flow through her fingers as she weeps. She tries not to think about the box under the floorboard that pulls away from the nails, where there is still a receiving blanket, and the frenzied drawings of a toddler. She tries not to think about the small knitted cap or the hand-written diary she kept during those nine long months. Or that awful note left on the living room table sixteen years later—the morning Adelaide awoke to an empty cabin, alone once again. And she tries not to think about the man—never think about the man. The stranger with those dark, bewitching eyes.

STOP!

Adelaide brushes away the last of her tears and listens to her ticking clock. She doesn't know why she has kept it all these years. Adelaide tells time by the sun and the shadows. Perhaps she has kept it so that there is something else to listen to.

Adelaide peers out the bedroom window toward the coop, seeking a glimpse of her chickens through the storm, but it seems they did not make it to shelter in time. She spots Henry's plum feathers just beyond the window frame, shivering beneath the eave of her cabin, and she pushes it open. Everything not too heavy to resist twists and sways in the wind. She listens for the mirror, but knows it is no longer there.

"Come on, Henry. Girls."

The chickens jostle around one another to be the first to perch on the open window. Moffit is triumphant and Adelaide ushers her into the warm bed. Zelda follows, collapsing onto the covers.

Henry stares at Adelaide, cocking his head to one side and shaking water from his crown.

"Well, that didn't do much good, did it? Get in here with us girls."

After a moment of deliberation, Henry perches on the window ledge.

Adelaide slides under the blanket while Zelda and Moffit scurry to the foot of her bed to roost on the post. They preen themselves and tuck their fatigued faces between their shoulders.

Henry is content to remain on the ledge, immune to Adelaide's insistent pats upon the mattress, so she pulls the rooster into her bed and latches the window closed.

Adelaide listens for evidence of her garden forager once the storm begins to slow, but sleep takes her quickly, and she believes it's only a dream when the gate of branches comes tumbling down.

3

The skin of a tomato lies outside the garden, and Adelaide kicks it over in the dirt. The barricade of branches has been disassembled and flung across the landscape. At her side, Henry perches atop the thickest one.

Inside the garden, Adelaide spots more devastation. She steps over the tomato plants, now ripped at their roots and splayed across the path. Her garden thief has tested the pumpkins, gouging the skin as though attempting to tear its way through with only its claws. One is smashed upon the ground, its guts strewn across the bed like sticky spiderwebs.

Outside the garden, the chickens have dispersed. Aside from a curious inspection of the stones and the bugs beneath, they are keeping their distance.

Adelaide fetches an onion from the dirt. Upon its flesh are the same unusual gouges found on the pumpkin, and she traces the pattern with her fingers.

Many years ago, Adelaide heard whispers of mountain lions in these woods, but those were usually dismissed by a wave of the hand and the suggestion of a myth. She's lived in the Blue Ridge Mountains for decades, and she's never seen a single shadow or paw print. And if there are big cats in her woods, surely there is more appetizing prey than melons and tomatoes. She scans her property, spotting Henry and the girls by the woodpile. Something must be done. And soon. Before her thief grows tired of vegetables.

She stares at the bizarre markings on the onion, imagining the lithe body of a mountain lion digging in her soil, rolling across the mulch, watching her chickens and waiting. Yes, she can see it now.

But how, Adelaide wonders, does one outsmart a mountain lion?

Once dark falls, Adelaide waits beneath the overhang of the roof. She tucks into the blackest part of the shadows and grips her flashlight, ready. At her feet is a metal bucket from the storage shed, half full of stones. Adelaide doesn't know if she will throw rocks at the cat or shake the bucket and let the racket scare him off. She must make her decision in the moment.

Adelaide can still recall how quiet it was, her first night under the stars. That was a long time ago—before finding the cabin, before the garden, before chickens—when her only shelter was a leaky orange tent, beneath the infinite swirl of the Milky Way. It was so quiet that she couldn't *hear*. Like a vacuum around her skull, vibrations through her brain. And a baritone hum that assaulted her ears for hours until she wept into the leaves, trying desperately to break the spell. She thought she had a bug in her ear, or a brain tumor, or some terrible disease that no one had ever heard of because no one would be as stupid as she, to go so deep into the Blue Ridge Mountains alone, where no one would ever find her body should she die *right then*.

She knows the truth now. It is a rare gift, an experience most will never know—the sound of true and utter *silence*. It is anything but quiet, and in the unprepared, it can inspire madness.

Adelaide squints into the darkness, but the harder she peers into the shadows, the less she can actually see. Certainly not the ideal conditions for stalking a night predator. Adelaide brings her fists to her eyes to buff away the gloom, and the metal flashlight bashes against her skull. Blood trickles down her face.

"Goddammit," she curses under her breath.

Adelaide places the flashlight at her feet and dabs the blood with her nightgown.

She's really losing it.

Here she is, in the middle of the woods, facing off against a mountain lion with nothing but a pail of rocks, and she can't even hold a flashlight without hurting herself. *This* is why she took a pocket full of pills to the river. It had been the right choice.

Now her garden is destroyed, her head is bloodied, she's sleep-deprived, stressed to high hell, and now her favorite nightgown is stained. And where's the goddamned flashlight?

She searches the dirt until her fingers touch metal and she wrangles the flashlight closer, slowly—*slowly*. She can't give away her position.

A noise from the garden. A growl? Maybe.

Adelaide presses the flashlight button and the path before her illuminates into a narrow golden rod.

Something moves through her garden.

Adelaide yelps, and the flashlight slips from her fingers once more, spinning across the dirt.

It's watching her, she knows it. She can't see it, but she can *feel* it, and she's learned not to doubt her instincts.

How fast can she run? She knows the answer before the thought is fully formed in her mind—not fast enough.

The rolling flashlight comes to a stop, shining against the corner of her wattle fence, small bits of light careening into the garden.

Dirt whirls through the air as the flashlight flickers—once, twice—before going dark.

Adelaide bangs it against her palm. Shakes it. Nothing.

And then she hears the growl.

A little like a hurricane, a little like a child wailing, a little like two rocks being ground together.

The growl is unwavering, surging toward Adelaide. Growing louder, or perhaps closer.

Adelaide has been spotted; she should run. But not yet. She wants to see the beast that has been ransacking her garden. *She needs to see it, will not leave until she sees it.*

Adelaide pushes away from the cabin—just a little—peering into the garden that once had a gate, and into the shadows. But then blood drips into her eye and she can see nothing at all. Adelaide stumbles forward and her foot catches the handle of the bucket. She collapses to the ground as stones spill from the pail with metallic clangs loud enough to rival her racing heart. The dirt, like small fragments of glass, tears at her fingertips.

The growl ceases. Adelaide swipes at the blood, looks all around, but her eyes burn, and her vision is muddled. A shadow rushes from the garden, pausing to appraise the old woman who is now panting and stumbling to her feet.

The wattle fence creaks with the weight of the beast. The moon is eclipsed by the height of the beast.

Adelaide does not throw a stone into the night. She does not look back to the garden, nor examine the wounds on her knees.

Adelaide runs.

Two nights pass before Adelaide can bring herself to stray far from the cabin.

The morning after the incident, she delivered a snack to the chickens, but then scampered back to the safety of her home. She has not gone outside to feed them since, but that was mere ceremony anyway—they get all they need from the forest.

This morning, Adelaide is relieved to see they've survived another night.

She had not seen the cat, not exactly, but she had *felt* it. Adelaide has no desire to leave this world in a torturous battle of tooth and claw.

"Keep watch over our girls, Henry," she whispers. "There's danger about."

The rooster chortles a whittled response. He, too, is hesitant to announce his presence.

The breeze carries a scent of something dewy and sweet, and Adelaide breathes it in. A little bit of decomposing leaves, a little bit of damp and compacted soil. And, today, a little bit of wood smoke—somewhere, a fire is burning.

Here, in the shadows of the Blue Ridge Mountains, her neighbors are few. There is a man who lives south of her, and brings mail to and from the nearest town for all the mountain folk. Just north of her, a young couple has begun building their vacation cabin—Adelaide will occasionally watch a shiny new pickup truck teeter past her cabin and up the road that skirts the mountain, hauling lumber and supplies.

And a few miles to the east is a small colony of people she tries to forget. They run the kind of farm that only thrives far from the watchful eyes of authorities. When the sun is hot and the wind is strong, Adelaide can smell the marijuana all the way down into her valley, as though with their stink, they have marked the forest as their own.

That's it!

Adelaide must get back to her garden right away. Why hadn't she thought of this earlier? She can't claim her territory with rocks and a flashlight. She has to speak the cat's language. *Scent.*

She knows now what must be done.

"Don't you judge me."

Henry, Zelda, and Moffit watch with curiosity as Adelaide lifts her dress and squats against the fence.

"You must understand," she continues, as her urine stains the soil, "this is the only way to talk to it."

She clenches midstream, and though her bladder demands release, Adelaide is a willful woman and will not allow for discourse, no matter how strong the argument. She squats against the nearest gatepost and splashes more of her scent.

"You don't want to be eaten by a mountain lion, do you?"

Moffit scampers to the post and kicks around in the moistened dirt, as though Adelaide may have dropped a few insects while she was at it.

The second post finely dusted, Adelaide moves from bed to bed, lifting her dress and dribbling her scent across the garden.

When she has finished, Adelaide looks to her chickens and shrugs. "At least you can say I've tried everything."

Henry bobs his head in agreement and saunters into the weeds by the compost pile. The girls follow, leaving Adelaide alone in the garden, surrounded by evaporating puddles of her own piss.

Night rolls in quickly, and Adelaide stands in the kitchen, staring at the little bottle of pills on the window ledge.

It was not so long ago that Adelaide fell while mending the fence. Maybe ten years ago, or eleven. She remembers the pain and the sound of her leg snapping when her ankle was caught beneath a tree limb. She remembers the long, torturous walk to her nearest neighbor, now long gone. And then the beeping of the monitors in the town hospital's surgical wing. The limp bag dripping god-knows-what into her bloodstream, and the monochromatic meals served under plastic. But she ate their food and said, "Yes, sir," and, "I will, ma'am," and, "Of course I have insurance," and she took their crutches and slipped out the exit doors, disappearing into the night, a bottle of pills rattling in her pocket.

The bed is cold and Adelaide's joints ache as she slips beneath the sheets. Somewhere in the forest a coyote begins to yip. Others join his song and she stays awake for as long as she can, listening to their ballad.

Adelaide thinks of her garden and all the vegetables lost, of her chickens and what might become of them should she leave this world before the garden thief has been banished, and the sound of the river when she dips her head beneath the surface.

Tonight, she does not think about the box under the floorboard.

Adelaide could have reassembled the garden gate before the sun went down, but that wouldn't be an accurate test of her scent theory. And there is a part of her, buried just below her fear of the animal's intentions and her anger over a trespasser in her garden, that wants to see if she can *win*.

The morning wind is chilly and carries with it the fetid smell of waste. Adelaide walks toward her garden with her hands held out before her, as if by blocking the breeze she can spare her nose the stench.

Smeared down the wooden post of the garden is the dark smudge of excrement.

"My god."

Adelaide creeps closer toward the smear, hand pressed to her mouth so she doesn't have to taste its odor. As soon as she crosses the garden perimeter, Adelaide sees the true havoc wreaked by the animal. Feces have been smeared across the garden beds, flung against the wattle fence, and even deposited directly onto her very last untouched pumpkin.

The animal must be nearby. The smell is fresh, the texture soft and not yet hardened by the morning sun. Adelaide takes a step back, her heel slipping on something slick and oily. She squeals, nearly tumbling to the ground, but it is a tomato. That's it. Only a tomato—the last of her crop.

Adelaide sprints out of the garden and into her cabin. The stink follows.

An idea germinates in Adelaide's mind. She tries to suppress it, but it takes root and flourishes, and simply cannot be ignored. There is a trap in the garden shed—one of those nasty metal ambushes with teeth like the devil coming up from the ground to swallow you whole. She used it once, a long time ago, when a bear was stalking her cabin in the night, killing her chickens and tearing at the wood siding. She had no choice. It was her or the bear. And no animal is going to run her from her home. She found its paw the next morning still clinging to the trap, chewed clean off at the ankle.

She'd tossed the paw into the river, and the trap into the storage shed. Never again, she said. But the trap had worked. The bear did not return.

The steel trap is an option, but a brutal and violent one. Surely there are less extreme solutions.

But it's reassuring to know that if things get ugly, she can always dig the trap from its resting place and take care of the beast once and for all.

4

Under the sink, behind the borax and the dishrags and the empty mason jars, Adelaide finds an old box of mousetraps.

Many of the traps are warped by moisture and time, but most still snap shut as intended. Adelaide smiles. Finally, an advantage.

The afternoon sun has baked each smear into a hardened ridge, but the stench is in the air, on her skin, in her hair. She will need a bath after this.

Adelaide lays each trap faceup—nothing wrong with a little pinch—across the garden, among the pathways and garden beds, and conceals them with soil.

She replaces a few of the larger branches at the entrance to deter her chickens and turns to find all three of them before her, eyes like searchlights scanning her feet.

"Stay out of the garden today," she warns them.

Moffit takes a step forward, defiant, and Adelaide kicks her foot. Three chickens scuttle through the air in a fury of feathers and displeasure. Only Henry looks back.

Adelaide disrobes and lays her clothes across the steps before walking to the river. She steps carefully over jagged rocks and twisted roots to slip into the water.

Winter is not kind to the elderly. The temperature has dropped, and the chill of the water shocks her skin, stiffens her joints.

Adelaide thinks of the mountain lion and laughs at her foolishness. Everything has spiraled so out of control. No one will want her little homestead when she is gone, as much as she may wish otherwise. *Of course* it belongs to the wild cats. And the squirrels and the coyotes and the birds and the chickens and all the other furred and winged critters. She's carved out a place for herself alongside the most untamed parts of the forest, but her time in this wild world has come to an end.

After her bath, she will dress, remove those silly mousetraps from the garden, and throw them straight into the deepest part of the river. In the morning, she will don her white skirt and her white sweater, and she will take her pills and take her leave. Responsibly. Alone, as always.

Adelaide is examining her reflection in the river when she spots motion from the corner of her eye. A plume of dust rises from the dirt road along the mountain base.

Someone is coming.

It is not the young couple hauling supplies in their shiny, new pickup truck. Nor is it the man who brings mail to his neighbors. There's only one other family on this side of the mountain, and Adelaide freezes, watching an old sedan draw closer to her driveway. Closer. Closer. And it turns.

Adelaide springs from the river and dashes to her cabin, covering her nakedness as best she can. Who is in the car? Why are they here? And what could they possibly want with a tired old crone like her?

Adelaide tugs her wet arms through a housedress as the knocks grow louder. A man peers through the smudged glass of her window, and she steps farther into the shadows.

A voice, young and slow, says, "Open the door. We know you're there."

We.

The knock comes again, deafening, insistent. No good has ever come of a knock on Adelaide's door.

"Come on lady. Just concerned neighbors out here is all. Just some questions."

His voice is smooth and pleasant, but Adelaide is not a young woman, and no longer so easily fooled. That velvet tone bears the unmistakable twinge of malevolence.

"Sonofabitch." Spoken under the breath—not to her, but to someone else.

If she can wage war against a mountain lion, she can surely handle this. Whatever *this* is.

Thunder erupts from her door as a fist strikes it, over and over, until Adelaide practically sprints forward to open the door to relieve the sound.

A young man stands before her in the light. Another stands just behind the first, kicking the dirt. She studies their faces. Waxy skin. Pores like sinkholes tunneling into their flesh. The man before her smiles, and Adelaide looks into his eyes to avoid staring at the fragments of his teeth.

In his eyes is something familiar, though she has never met this person. But still, within those wells of chestnut brown lies something she has seen before. She takes a step back, grasping the door frame. The man laughs.

"You alright? You gonna fall?" he asks.

"No."

"No, you not alright? Or no, you ain't gonna fall?"

The reek of his breath quickly fills the space between them, and she looks to the man in shadow. His face, so similar to the first.

"You hear me?"

Adelaide tries to speak but her tongue fills the back of her throat. She holds her hand up to indicate that she does not require assistance.

The young man stares, his eyes roaming down her body, slow and lingering. Adelaide looks down to see that the wetness of her body has melded the fabric to her flesh. The folds of her skin, her areolae, even the age spots on her hips, are fully visible in the sunlight. Adelaide shakes the fabric from her body.

"Well," he coughs and continues, "we're here because there's been some damage to our farm."

An image of feces smeared across the garden flashes through her mind.

"You ain't been up to our farm, have you?" he asks.

She shakes her head. "No."

"I s'pose not."

He scans her body again, and Adelaide shuffles closer to the door frame.

"But you never know 'bout people sometimes."

At last, the second man speaks. "You a witch?"

Adelaide can't help but laugh, though she'd prefer to knee him in the crotch, grind some salt into his eyes, and send him home with a good story. He does not smile, and both men stare openly, awaiting her response.

The young men standing before her are clearly brothers. It's in the eyes. Something dark. Bewitching. The two men seem to mirror each other's movements. When Brother #1 shifts his weight to the left foot, Brother #2 shifts to the right, as though ricocheting from the same point in opposite directions.

When she does not respond, Brother #2 speaks again. "People say it is all. You should know people say it."

Adelaide nods slowly and looks to her hands, alabaster, cracked. The young have always constructed extravagant explanations for things they don't understand. She wants to tell him that she is simply an old woman who lives in the woods. There are no fairy tales to be found here. No folklore. She wants to tell him that *youth* is the true magic of the world—so much to create, so much to destroy—and by the time he realizes the truth of that, he and his brother will be witches, too. But she says none of this.

"What do you want?" she asks.

"Told you. There's been some damage to our farm."

"I don't know anything about your farm. I'm sorry."

She begins to close the door, but Brother #1 places his hand against it and leans forward.

"You ever seen somethin' out in those woods you shouldn't?" he asks. His voice is low, as though he may be overheard.

Adelaide falters, but manages to say, "Just a cat is all."

He smiles, his teeth like gravel at the edge of a cliff. "Ain't no cat."

His eyes bore into her. She wills him to take a step back, but he does not.

"Somethin's been sniffin' 'round our property. You know what we grow up there?"

"No," she lies.

He nods. "Well, we can't have somethin' tearin' up our crops. Family land n' all." He cranes his neck and stares into her home. "You got a husband? I'd like to talk to 'im."

"No husband," she says, and regrets it immediately.

Again, that false smile. "I s'pose not. Children?"

Adelaide swallows the stone that's been growing in her throat. "No."

He smiles. "I hear you got a daughter."

"DO YOU SEE ANY CHILDREN HERE?" she bellows, and finally—*finally*—he releases her door and steps back into the dirt.

"Okay, okay, no need to yell." He laughs, the sound like a barking dog. He stares at Adelaide in a silence that broadens and thickens between them until Adelaide fears she might drown within it.

Brother #2 speaks up from behind. "Can we go now?"

Brother #1 dips his head in courtesy, a demonstration of his fine manners. "Ma'am."

Adelaide shuts the door—a little too hard—and the small, round mirror tumbles from the wall. It does not shatter, but the sound echoes through the cabin, and Adelaide feels it in her bones.

She plucks the mirror from the floor and raises it to the light. Her eyes are crazed, her nostrils flared. She traces a new wrinkle along her chin. Such a silly old woman she is. Those young men weren't admiring her body—they were shocked by it. Adelaide had been in fear of what they might do to her, but she holds no sexual appeal to those men. No longer any need to worry about a man entering her home, eyes frenzied and aglow, pinning her down, ripping her clothes. Time has made her immune.

She hangs the mirror back on its nail and walks to the kitchen window to make sure that the men have indeed left her property.

Their car is still parked in her driveway, three figures inside.

We.

Her empty belly tilts.

One brother sits at the wheel, the other in the back. But there is another man. Thinner. Older. He leans forward in the passenger seat, staring at her cabin as the two young men are locked in conversation. He smiles, and Adelaide nearly cries out. She drops to the floor, throwing herself against the cabinets and out of his view.

Like her, he is old now. His shoulders hunched, his body fragile. But those eyes—she could never forget those eyes. Even so many years later.

Adelaide crouches against the floorboards and wills the car to be gone from her woods.

Why is he still here?

She pleads for the men to drive away.

What is he planning?

She wraps her arms around her knees like a little girl, and imagines stillness and peace surrounding her home in a tight circle, protecting her from wickedness. And then she wonders, if she stands right now, will the old man be at her window, his dark, bewitching eyes pressed against the glass?

When Adelaide finds the strength to stand, there is no man at her window. And there is no car in her driveway. She takes a deep breath and steadies herself against the sink. The forest is silent, as if it never even happened.

She envisioned it, and now everything is as it should be. Perhaps she is a witch after all.

Wind gusts against her cabin, and from deep in the woods, an incessant howl.

Adelaide has given up on slumber and instead lights the fireplace—the first of the season. In years past, this moment has been a celebration. Tonight, it is a vigil.

She draws her curtains for fear of being watched, pulls some pickled carrots from her cupboard, and listens to the *tick-tick-tick* of her clock. It may as well be laughing at her.

There are a plethora of nighttime sounds in the Blue Ridge Mountains. There are crickets and cicadas, mice and deer, creaky trees, and crooning owls, and other sounds that Adelaide has heard all her life but never known the origin. They are simply the sounds of the forest, running together in an orchestra of noise, thick and singular. Most nights, she doesn't even notice it. But tonight is different. Tonight, Adelaide analyzes every creak, every whoosh. And no matter how close she inches toward the fire it does not eradicate her chill.

Adelaide plucks a carrot from the jar, licks the juice, and then crushes it against the roof of her mouth. For a moment, she believes she hears the sound of a car engine idling toward her cabin, but it is merely a spot of thunder that rumbles once more before falling away.

No, there will be no sleep tonight.

Behind the sofa, under the floorboard that pulls away from the nails, a box lies beneath. Adelaide thought she would never look inside it again, but tonight she finds herself wondering about the colors. The blanket—is it white with pink stripes or pink with white stripes? The small knitted cap—is it lemon yellow or butter yellow? There is a small stuffed toy as well. She nearly forgot. Is it an elephant or a hippo? My god, how the mind loses the small things.

A screech startles Adelaide from her thoughts, and the jar of carrots falls from her grasp, rolling across the room as she stands before the glowing embers of the fireplace. From outside her cabin, a sound like a whip cracking through the night, and then silence. Another crack, and another shriek.

Adelaide rushes to the kitchen window and pushes aside the curtain. The trees sway and jostle as something moves through them, fleeing her garden.

The mousetraps! She forgot to remove them this afternoon. Adelaide gasps. *That poor creature.* She stares into the night, but everything is once again still, aside from the breeze rushing down from the mountain.

Adelaide does not know what has woken her. Dawn is still hours away—she can tell by the opaque black beyond the windows. Inside, her cabin is warm, the embers in the fireplace still smoldering red. The ticking of her clock echoes like a mousetrap. *Snap-snap-snap.* Adelaide twitches with the passing of every second.

And then a sound. Hushed, but close, like something scraping against her cabin walls.

Adelaide bolts upright and steadies herself against the sofa. She's still sleeping. *Must* be sleeping.

Something gallops past her living room window, and Adelaide ducks. It was large, low to the ground, running on all fours.

The beast.

She spins to face the kitchen and sees its silhouette rush past the drapes.

It's circling her house.

Adelaide crawls toward her bedroom, but the creature is already there, a hulking shadow pressed against the glass. Pushing. Thumping. Looking for a way inside.

Adelaide drops to the floor, and dust floods her lungs. She coughs. So loud. *So loud.* The beast will surely hear her and come crashing through the glass to tear the tendons from her neck, splatter her home with her own scalding blood. She braves a peek at the bedroom window, but the condensation renders the creature shapeless and undefinable.

Her clock continues to tick, the sound like an admonishment, ashamed at what she has allowed to escalate. What she has brought on herself. The clock chastises, *tsk-tsk-tsk*.

She has lost this battle with the mountain lion. If that's what it is. Visibility was obscured, but still, she did not see a cat outside her window—cats don't gallop. She thinks of the young man who stood before her, just this morning, interrogating her about an animal destroying his crops. That look in his eyes when she said it was a cat. And he had said something—what had he said?

The creature is outside her front door now, and Adelaide pinches her knuckles, waiting for whatever comes next.

It's all led up to this. She just had to fight, didn't she? Had to win. Couldn't let it go, goddammit.

The creature rubs its body against the door, the coarse bristle of fur on wood.

A tapping, gentle.

Pushing.

What is it doing?

The knob rattles.

Did she lock it?

Yes, she definitely locked it. But still, the creature is turning the knob somehow. Impossible. The metal latch shifts back and forth as the animal tests it from the other side. Please hold, she hopes—*begs*—and she hears her own voice somewhere in the distance chanting, "Oh my god, oh my god, oh my god."

The beast slams its weight against the old wooden door. Adelaide stands. Her legs are warm and wet, and she realizes she has released her bladder.

And just as suddenly as it began, it stops.

The shadowy figure darts past the living room window, and Adelaide listens as the creature tunnels away from her cabin and into the woods. A howl fractures the night, like a wolf drawn to celebrate the full moon. But that was no wolf.

Adelaide is once again left with the silence, and the flood of a memory she'd been seeking. She remembers what Brother #1 had said, just this morning as he stood on her doorstep. Adelaide said it was a cat destroying the crops. He'd looked at her cross and he'd said something. She couldn't remember his words before, but she does now. Adelaide remembers *exactly* what he said.

Ain't no cat.

5

Adelaide lifts the corrugated metal lid from the cube of her storage bin and drops it to the ground. The chickens scatter in a flurry of startled squawks. She locates the chain snaking out from a cluttered corner where just beneath an old muddied tarp sits the steel trap, glinting and ready.

Adelaide wrestles a rake from the shed, lifting it high above her head. Henry peers at her from the corner of the wattle fence.

"It's okay, Henry. We're gonna catch us a monster tonight, what do you say?"

Henry cocks his head, but otherwise remains silent.

"I thought you'd say that. No, no, you stay back. I'll handle it."

The rake swings before her as Zelda and Moffit join the discussion.

"Don't think about it. You'll be asleep anyway, locked up tight. You won't see a thing."

Adelaide enters the garden and uses the tines of the rake to scrape dried feces from a post. The girls investigate but find nothing of interest.

"Don't look at me that way. I've tried everything else."

Adelaide leans upon the rake, admiring the patterns of morning light advancing up the path.

She clears the melon bed—or what used to be the melon bed, now just an empty mound—of a hardened lump of excrement.

Despite the chill, a bead of sweat rolls down Adelaide's jaw.

She drags the rake along a corner bed, choked with weeds, and a pop of green foliage tangles in the tines. "Oh Henry! Look at this!"

The rooster toddles closer, balancing on his legs like fragile twigs.

Adelaide burrows her fingers within the soil, unearthing a small, firm potato. She gasps.

"I just assumed . . . but I was wrong! How wonderful to be wrong."

Adelaide tunnels into the dirt again, and once she has dug the entire plant from the ground, she finds herself with six small, perfect potatoes. Plenty for one old woman. At last, a blessing.

Adelaide tucks the spuds into her skirt pockets for later and marches to the shed to retrieve the steel trap. This is the right choice. And the universe has granted its approval as well, authenticated in potatoes.

This is it. What it's all come down to.

Adelaide versus beast.

The trap is heavier than Adelaide remembers, and she struggles to lift it from the shed. When she finally heaves the contraption to the ground, Adelaide collapses beside it, tumbling into a plume of dirt. The chickens scatter as she lurches toward the garden, dragging the trap behind her.

By the time Adelaide has poled the trap, set it, and camouflaged it with weeds, the sky has already darkened to a muted pumpkin orange. Adelaide massages her lower back, her fingers, each knuckle a sharp little acorn within her flesh. The metal teeth of the trap have scratched both her shins, and soil is caked in the wounds.

Adelaide walks to the river to rinse the abrasions, but the water is too high, and the current too strong, to fully submerge. She leans against the largest rocks, splashing water across her shins. The wind is bitter, and it nips at her skin, tousling her long gray hair from its bun.

Adelaide stares into the darkening sky, a spattering of stars already visible.

She smells it before she sees it. Fire.

In the distance, billows of white smoke reach high into the evening sky, their fingers twisting and coiling in the wind as they extend up, up, up. The smell is of ash and greenery. Crops. Thin flashlight beams arc across distant trees, and the shouts of men dissipate into the air before she can assess their words. Adelaide never likes to see smoke. It is a reminder that she is not alone in these woods.

Adelaide resists the urge to flee the riverside.

She is fine, she tells herself. *Fine.* She takes a moment to smooth her clothes and brush the water from her legs as vultures circle in perilous halos above her, twisting and dipping through the sky.

A branch snaps and crashes to the forest floor on the other side of the river. Adelaide flinches, and grasps her chest. She's being foolish. But even still, she wants to go back to the cabin.

Now.

Adelaide runs along the worn path through the trees, collapses through her front door, and jams the bolt into place.

Despite the warmth of the cabin, her bedsheets are cold, and she shivers beneath them, thin and tired, listening to the calls of owls. On evenings like this, one can hear for miles.

Hounds bay in the distance, the sound growing faint, loud, and then faint once more. The dogs move quickly through the forest, hunting, seeking.

Adelaide stares at the marks on her ceiling, the stains like reishi mushrooms clustered and flourishing in the death of a fallen tree.

The dogs don't stop hunting until the first rays of dawn break over the mountain ridge. Adelaide knows this because she has not slept.

The ticking clock is the only noise in the cabin this morning. Like a friend with a secret, it whispers, *pst-pst-pst*.

If Adelaide didn't know better, she might call out a greeting, as if someone were hiding in the shadows. She senses it in the air—the feeling of being seen. Noticed. Adelaide smiles. She can still recall what it was like to have someone waiting for her in the morning. It's a thought she hasn't entertained in many years. Not since her daughter left. That stage of Adelaide's life has passed, and there are no second chances. But as she walks to the kitchen, she throws a glance over her shoulder, just in case.

The potatoes are lined up on the counter. She squeezes one, testing the firmness, but this is mere distraction. Adelaide faces the window above the sink, but it's fogged with condensation, and she cannot see into the garden.

She leans over the counter to wipe it away. Pauses. Her fingers hover before the window as little droplets cascade down, painting strokes of visibility. She takes a deep breath to still her heart and places her hand on the glass. No going back now.

Adelaide swipes away the haze, straining to see down the path and into the garden that once had a gate.

The trap is empty.

Adelaide scowls at the barren trap still cloaked in weeds and glistening with moisture.

The forest is quite a sight this time of year—a kaleidoscope of colors glittering from every damp surface. But by her feet, as if by brutal betrayal of nature itself, the glint of a stainless steel tooth.

"Out of here, all of you."

The chickens scatter in all directions and spill into the yard.

"Not safe," she says to the chickens, pointing to the place where the trap is hidden. "Not today," she says mostly to herself.

Adelaide had hoped to take her final walk down to the river this morning with a pocket full of pills and the promise of eternal rest. But now it seems that eternal rest will have to wait one more day. *Just one more day*. She's delayed long enough. If the thief eludes capture once more, Henry will have to protect the girls on his own.

Adelaide replaces the branches at the garden entrance to deter the chickens, and walks back to her home. She can practically smell the potatoes from here.

The kindling in the fireplace ignites, and warmth pours into the small cabin. A few roasted potatoes sound like a fine feast this morning. The one thing the garden thief hasn't devoured. Her one small victory.

Adelaide hums as she scrubs the soil from the bounty. She doesn't remember many songs from her youth, but she carries the melody of a song created on the spot as she plucks a potato from the counter and carves away petite bits of roots and eyes.

Such a beautiful morning. If she were to handpick a single day to be her last, it would be a day exactly like this. Warm and cold. Light and dark. Wet and dry. Adelaide laughs and slices another cleansed potato into chunks. A glorious day to be alive.

The blade skips across Adelaide's finger and she flinches, her breath caught behind her teeth. Nothing serious, but she should be more mindful. She is reaching for the final potato when she hears the trap slam shut.

The metal teeth clang together, and the beast unleashes a howl unlike any she's ever heard, before falling silent.

Adelaide doesn't want to go outside. She doesn't want to look out the window. The blade trembles in her fist and she places it on the cutting board.

The sound startles her as it rings through the trees once more—a horror of a scream, an anomaly of a scream. As if it is right outside her window. This is not a cat in her garden. Nor a coyote. And a bear, no matter how frightened, would never make a sound like that.

The beast begins to wail.

She wills it to die. *Begs* it to die. Adelaide grinds her fists into her ears, but it does not stanch the sound. It is everywhere—in the walls, on the floor, within her flesh. She fumbles through the kitchen drawer and rustles through the utensils, casting spatulas and whisks to the floor.

The wailing ceases. An entire forest grown quiet.

Perhaps she won't need the cleaver after all.

But then she sees it, tangled in a hoop of plastic measuring cups. She snatches it into her fist and thrusts it toward the window as though the threat alone may suffice.

Adelaide spots movement in her garden. The beast is dragging the chain toward the fence—it's trying to escape! The steel chain grates against the wattle fence. And then the screaming resumes—a barbarity of a scream, an abomination of a scream.

She regrets everything.

6

Adelaide leaves the front door open as she descends the steps. The screaming has stopped. But just beyond the garden perimeter, other noises: snorting, grunting, shuffling.

The branches lie across the ground, and Adelaide steps carefully over them—*don't fall, don't fall.*

She holds the cleaver out before her like a battle-ax and approaches the spot where she laid the trap. The rod of the trap is still locked in the earth, the chain pulled taut across the garden and disappearing into shadow. Fractured boughs of willow litter the ground.

The beast bellows and kicks at the wattle fence. The thicker wood splinters, the lesser wood explodes. Fragments of pine and willow pepper Adelaide's face, and she shields her eyes with the blade.

Adelaide hears a whine like an abridged yawn. Hushed whispers like the passing of breath through gritted teeth.

She steps carefully over the branches—*don't fall, don't fall.*

She must be cautious. No accidents. No noise.

She grips the cleaver tighter. She knows what must be done and can delay no longer. She is better than this. She's hunted before. Skinned, processed. This is no different. *No different.*

Something shuffles through the leaves, and Adelaide hears a noise like a raspy cough in the back of the throat. And then another sound—higher, lighter—answers the first.

There's more than one.

She must do it.

Now.

Before she loses her nerve.

Whether she dies tomorrow in the river eddy, or right here by claw and by tooth, she is ready.

Adelaide spins around, raises the blade and charges through the shadows. Tears spill from her eyes. Her bun unravels, strands of silver rope twisting behind her. The trees stretch in her periphery—they, too, eager to see what has sprung the mighty steel jaws.

Adelaide's breath catches in her throat, choking and wheezing, much like a beast herself, when she comes upon it. She skids to a stop, landing on her tailbone, as the cleaver spins from her grasp and disappears into the trees.

She cannot believe what she is seeing. And she cannot look away.

Before her, covered in mud, skin thick as a coconut husk, is a *woman.*

She faces away from Adelaide, snarling over her shoulder, kicking at the dirt as if in tantrum. The woman whips her head and spits, hisses through orange teeth, her face half hidden beneath a wedge of matted hair. The woman is wild, nude, her spine protruding like a staircase. The steel teeth of the trap impale her ankle, and she sits in a pool of her own blood.

Adelaide steps forward. "Are you o—"

The woman howls, spits. Strands of hair tangle in her mouth and between her teeth, though she takes little notice. Adelaide takes a step back, and the woman turns away, silent, as if Adelaide were not there at all. She curls around an object in her arms, but Adelaide cannot see past the broad hulk of her shoulders.

Adelaide advances slowly, skirting the trees for cover. The woman, as though sensing the threat with her very skin, emits a low guttural drone that causes the air in the clearing to throb.

"Hello?" Adelaide calls out, though it issues as a whisper from her lips.

The growl intensifies, and Adelaide regrets losing her grip on the cleaver.

"I can help you," she says.

The woman ignores this, staring intently at the thing in her lap.

"Let me remove the trap for you. Please. I'm so sorry."

The woman swings her head toward Adelaide. Her brows, thick and unkempt, grow to a crescendo between her black eyes. Her soiled teeth protrude from parched lips.

Adelaide holds her breath, and in her head, she hears the words spoken mere days ago, like a prophecy: *ain't no cat.*

No cat indeed.

The woman locks her eyes on Adelaide.

"What have you got there?"

The sun emerges from behind the clouds, painting the woman with light. Her body is embroidered with dozens of fresh scratches and old scars. One could trace constellations across her skin.

Tucked within her arms is a swatch of fur. An animal?

The wild woman pulls herself closer to the fence, and from beneath the woman's elbow, Adelaide spots a small foot, dirt caked between wriggling pink toes.

Dear god.

Adelaide rushes toward the woman, no longer hesitant, no longer fearful, and shoves her shoulder aside. The wild woman shuffles backward, wailing, shackled by her injured ankle.

Folded within the woman's arms are two naked children, their small black eyes peering up at Adelaide.

Before Adelaide can determine her next move, the woman lunges forward. The children leap from her arms to scamper for cover as their mother sinks her foul, stained teeth into Adelaide's leg.

7

Adelaide collapses onto the kitchen floor, cradling her throbbing calf.

Outside, the wild woman continues to roar, more mountain lion than human after all.

The bite marks are gaping caverns in her calf, and she scours her cabinets for a bottle of peroxide. Adelaide did not send a supply list last season—there was no want, no need, where she was heading—and her supplies have dwindled. She pushes aside half-bottles of vinegar and linseed oil until she discovers a forgotten bottle of bleach. At least it's something.

Outside, the wild woman screams and Adelaide flinches, spilling bleach across the wood floor. Already the color blanches. Adelaide breathes through the woman's scream, wills it to end. But it continues, as if the wild woman has inhaled all the oxygen from the forest, collapsing the mighty trees, expelling it in one ferocious trumpet call. Adelaide cannot breathe until it stops. She mustn't. She won't. She holds her breath until her lungs are just another heartbeat pushing and throbbing against her ribs.

When the morning dips into silence once more, Adelaide exhales in a frantic rush and looks to the ceiling. Before she can change her mind, she closes her eyes, and splashes bleach across her wounded leg.

Adelaide cries out. She did not expect pain like this, and her scream catches in her throat. Her leg is a cavern of flame, rolling fire, blue and orange, cinder and log. Will the regrets never cease?

And then the morning goes black.

Adelaide wakes to the sound of Henry. She smiles at his garbled cry until the ache in her leg reminds her that there are more pressing matters demanding her attention. The light coming through her window is amber— the sun will be setting soon, and she has already lost so much time.

The skin of her calf is clean and pink, but the holes are black. A crooked little nest of incisors and canines.

The pill bottle mocks her from the window ledge, as if to say: *stop complaining, you had your chance.*

Adelaide pauses at her door, willing Henry to be quiet as he chortles another call to the waning sun. She hauls her tired body past the garden and jostles her hands as though dread can be flung from the body like river water. Her eyes are trained on the corner of the wattle fence, beyond which the wild woman is surely already aware of her approach.

Grasping the fence for support, Adelaide edges closer to the corner of her garden, craning for another look.

She is there—*right there.*

The wild woman watches Adelaide emerge from the shadows. Her teeth are long and unclenched, and from her throat a growl rattles forth so low that Adelaide can't be sure if there is sound at all, or merely vibration.

The children are gone. *Where are the children?*

Splinters of willow branches lay in heaps across the tree line. Blood pools in a small trench between the fence and the woman.

Adelaide peers through the shadows and detects two shadowy forms shifting behind their mother's curved spine.

Adelaide wishes she had someone to call, consult. If this were a fallen tree, she would know what tools to retrieve. If this were a broken porch step, she would know how to repair it. But there is no instruction manual for dealing with a feral human.

Adelaide clasps her hands to her face and weeps. She is done. Her reign is finished. She knows nothing; she never did.

Adelaide blinks away her tears long enough to meet the wild woman's gaze. She expects ferocity, but what she receives is so much more.

Reflected in the woman's eyes is concern. Adelaide wipes her face dry as the two women of the forest watch each other. Adelaide sees unexpected things in the face of the wild woman: the eyes of a worry-wart, furrows of anxiety etched into her forehead, creases sliding down her young face. Laugh lines. Adelaide gasps—this woman knows joy. She did not expect that. Behind the woman's torso, little fingers inch across her ribs and clasp onto her breast. She shakes herself free and the fingers disappear behind her back once more.

Adelaide raises her hand. "Hello there," she whispers.

The wild woman recoils, but does not attack, does not growl.

"Adelaide is my name," she says, patting her chest. "Adelaide."

The wild woman flexes her fingers but makes no move to raise her arm or speak a word. Behind her, the children begin to chatter. She swats a small backside and the children quiet down, contenting themselves with plucking bugs from their mother's hair. Each insect receives a cursory examination before being flung into the brush. If Henry and the girls were braver, there would be a squirming feast at their feet right now.

The sorting of insects seems to calm the wild woman. Her shoulders slouch, and despite the steel clutching her ankle, she shows no sign of pain. Her children burrow their carrot fingers through her hair as though she were a lioness. Every few minutes, one of the children lightly touches their forehead to hers. Adelaide knows about butterfly kisses and Eskimo kisses, but now she has learned about wild woman kisses. It feels good to learn something new.

Adelaide decides she will stay quiet by the little family and see if they might come to accept her presence. If that were to happen, she could loosen the trap, pry the jaws from the woman's ankle. It would be painful. Torturous, even. But Adelaide would not be harmed if she were understood to be a friend.

With a plan in place, Adelaide goes silent. The stones settle between her hips, and she fusses with her dress until most of it is tucked beneath, forming a thin cushion between her skin and the rocks.

And she waits.

Just before sunset, when only the palest bands of pink and violet light the sky, the wild woman closes her eyes. Adelaide plucks grass and flicks one strand after another, trying to keep her mind occupied, awake, ready.

Two pairs of eyes peer out from behind their sleeping mother's shoulder, and the children giggle as they watch a piece of grass flutter through the air. It seems they want to play.

Adelaide flicks another strand, sending it higher this time, arcing over the wild woman. The children drop to their hands and knees, and chase it through the brush. Their giggles grow louder, and Adelaide must be drunk on the fumes of bleach-burnt flesh, because now she is giggling, too.

The children begin to move slower, their knees tracing lines on the ground as they circle each other.

Adelaide has spent so much time playing with the children that she has nearly forgotten what must be done. She looks to the wild woman collapsed in the bloodstained dirt beneath her. It could be days before she accepts Adelaide's help, and neither of them have days to spare. With the wild woman asleep, Adelaide needs a new plan. A good one, and fast.

One of the children crawls over its mother's good leg and collapses into her chest, poking a finger through her matted hair. The wild woman strokes the child's head but does not fully wake.

Adelaide yawns, inhaling the moist air that tastes like soil and steel. And a little like blood.

When the other child stands, Adelaide sees that this one is a little boy. He follows his sister into the cradle of his mother's arms and falls fast asleep, a dirty thumb in his mouth.

And just like that, Adelaide is once again alone.

Adelaide watches the sleeping family from her kitchen window. Hers was a quiet retreat, and they did not wake. She'd wanted to stay. She'd wanted to curl up next to them and keep them safe until morning. Until she came up with a plan. A *real* plan. But she also needed a moment to think.

The wild family, a heap of feet, bowed heads, and tangled arms, doesn't appear cold, though even inside the cabin, Adelaide shivers. She imagines there is a warmth much heartier than a thick blanket or a roaring fire. And she imagines that must be lovely.

Just below her view of the children sits the little amber bottle of pills, a mountain of white disks inside. She opens the lid, sticks her nose into the opening and inhales. She smells the pills like a woman on a diet might whiff a chocolate cake. The scent is medicinal, which she expects, but beneath that base note, she detects others. Cream. Metal. A hint of oil. A top note of egg. Adelaide is a certified Suicide Sommelier as she swirls the pills in the bottle, watching them crest and fall over one another. They are waiting for her, and she knows it. She wants to give herself over to them, and she will—she tells herself this every day—but today is *still* not the day. Adelaide shoves the cap back onto the bottle and slams it against the porcelain sink, over and over. She throws the bottle across the cabin, and it lands in the corner of the living room.

Adelaide knows what she must do, and she pulls a pad and pen from a drawer.

She taps the pen, staring at those crisp, blue lines embedded across the page, mocking her hesitance, her fear. Once she writes it, it is done. Final. But she must stop convincing herself that she can control her own life. That belief is as mythological as her mountain lion.

And so she starts with basics.

Hydrogen Peroxide

Large bandages

Batteries

Window cleaner

Toilet paper

Washing soap

Canned goods (anything is fine. Whatever is convenient.)

Powdered milk

Matches

Lantern oil

Tea

Honey

Adelaide appraises her list. A little less than was requested last time. But there are still some additional supplies Adelaide will need, and she isn't sure if they require context. She decides that she is required to give no such explanations, and she continues.

Baby formula (powdered)

Baby bottles

Jars of baby food (as many as you can pack)

Cloth diapers

Adelaide searches her mind for anything else she might need. But her years of dealing with children feels like another life, and one she was only barely a part of.

She signs her name, Adelaide, before scratching it out. She takes a breath and signs "Mom." Below that she writes, in less formal handwriting, "I love you."

She hesitates before writing one more line—one last frivolous line—but once it is on the paper, in ink, Adelaide nods her approval.

"I know you are very busy with your own life, but if you are so inclined to bring a little something extra, please let it be a bottle of wine."

Adelaide folds her supply list and licks a stamp, pressing it into a yellowing envelope. She then adds another, in case postage has increased since her last stamp order, and slips out her door, past the garden and the sleeping family beyond, and treks up her gravel driveway toward the mountain road. It will be dark soon, and she must hurry.

She stares at her mailbox, an old rusty thing that no longer has a clasp. The lid hangs open like a ravenous mouth, and her hands shake as she stuffs the envelope down its dark throat. She raises the flag for the kind man who tends to his neighbors' correspondence, and walks away before she thinks better of it.

Adelaide removes the shovel from the storage shed, and takes a moment to catch her breath before hauling it toward the garden.

The children are by the tree line, a few feet away from their mother, stretching and turning into each other for warmth. The wild woman lies on her side, her bloodied limb protruding from the grip of metal teeth.

Adelaide creeps closer, mindful to avoid stepping on any branches that may signal her approach.

A quick jab and a twist, and the wild woman will be free. That's all it will take. And then she will help the woman stand and lead her to the cabin. She will tend to the mother's wounds, help care for the children . . .

Adelaide pauses in the clearing.

But what happens then? How will she coax them into the house? How will she build trust with this feral woman? How will she care for the woman's injury if she doesn't have even a simple bottle of peroxide?

Adelaide is unprepared for this onslaught of self-doubt, as one final question darts into her mind: What if the wild woman kills her?

It is certainly a possibility, and one she hadn't considered. Not since she mistakenly thought she was dealing with a mountain lion. Yes, this dirty naked woman right here at her feet could kill her.

Adelaide has not yet built a rapport with the wild woman, but neither can she waste any more precious time. She spots an opening in the jaws of the trap. This is where she will drive the shovel—right there, just below her ankle bone, where no additional harm will come to the woman. She will do it.

Right now.

Now.

NOW.

The wild woman opens her eyes and Adelaide cannot move. She is frozen, watching the woman part her lips, baring those orange teeth, canines and incisors as rusted as the mailbox flag.

Adelaide was wrong. This is not a woman she can trust to live in her home. This is, indeed, the mountain lion that destroyed her crops, desecrated her property, and terrorized her home.

In the shortest of moments, the wild woman has once again become the beast.

Adelaide mourns the quick reflexes of her youth, and she chances a glimpse at the children. Their hair is a mud slick of tangles, soil, and leaves. A toe twitches, a tongue lolls. They continue to dream, unaware of the events unfolding just above them.

The wild woman hunches her shoulders, the tendons in her neck stiffening. Her elbows bend and she crouches low to the ground, growling, spitting. But she does not move. Not yet.

There is electricity between the two women. Watching, evaluating, planning.

From the other side of her house, a chortle in the air. The chickens. Adelaide wills them back to sleep. To stay put. Silent. Away. Everything.

This was a mistake. A series of tragic and misguided mistakes. She is in over her head. Drowning. Lost on her own land. The river calls to her, the sound like an angel. *Adelaide,* the river whispers. *Lay it down. Lay it all down and come home.*

Henry trills into the night, and the wild woman turns toward the sound.

Before Adelaide can think—before she can stumble over another failed plan—she sprints toward the children.

Adelaide hurls the shovel over her shoulder as the wild woman launches from her position, heels drilling into the mud, fists like curled talons aimed at Adelaide. The chain links clack together, the chord ringing through the air like a battle cry. Adelaide barely hears it, barely sees anything through the tunnel of her sight. Her nightgown clutches at her ankles, tugs at her shins.

A clang rings through the night as the chain reaches its length, and the wild woman's scream splits Adelaide's head in two.

The children jolt awake, their faces contorting into puzzles of fright, as she rushes toward them. But surprise has given Adelaide the advantage. She throws her weight against the children, and scoops them up, like fat little chickens, one bare bottom in the crook of each elbow.

They cry out to their mother, reaching over Adelaide's shoulders, barking mutilated sounds and stunted syllables into the sky. Their arms tangle in her hair as they thrust their open palms toward their mother.

Adelaide does the only thing that makes sense in such a senseless situation. She runs. Back to her cabin. Back to warmth and safety, where every corner of every room is practical and predictable.

A little boy at the window, face flattened to the glass, clouds blooming from the depths of moist lungs. Croaking. Spitting. Wailing. Flat palms pounding. Knees locked and toes curling. Dirty fingers tearing at the ledge of the window frame. Blood on fingertips. Coughing. Voice cracking but still strong.

Another—a girl—hugging her own elbows. Rocking. Head behind her brother's knees. Eyes tightly shut. Rocking. Rocking. Feet twisting. A squeak, barely registered. Covering her face. Parting her hair. One eye on Adelaide. A puddle of urine beneath her small frame.

And Adelaide, watching, sweating. Her eyes, wide and nearly sightless. She gasps. Scared, wildly scared. Clutching her knees. She, too, rocking. Rocking. The room spinning. The wood floor beneath her feet like home at last, if only for a moment. She watches the windows, one by one. Listening. Waiting.

The room spins faster. Her chest tightens. From the lantern on the side table, light as bright as an emergency flare reflects against the glass, stinging her eyes. Adelaide would speak words if her lips weren't numb. And then everything blurs as the room turns to gray, then white, then black.

The howls continue outside long after Adelaide has fainted on the sofa.

When Adelaide wakes, her eyelids are too heavy to open, her limbs too sore to move, so she lies on her sofa and she listens.

Outside, the wild woman is loud and frightened, her shouts echoing through the small cabin.

Adelaide forces open an eye and peers across her living room.

The children are still there. It wasn't a dream.

They watch the empty place beyond the window as somewhere outside, their mother cries for them. The little globes of their heads turn left and then right. It would be in perfect unison were it not for their tendency to pull away from each other, as though ricocheting from the same point in opposite directions.

A nonverbal communication passes from the girl to her brother, almost imperceptible. He begins to cry.

More sounds from outside, different from before. Shuffling, pushing, pulling. And then the blast of metal striking metal.

A scream.

The children plaster themselves to the glass as stones and sticks slam against the walls, the window.

The wild woman barks a dozen strange sounds into the night sky.

And then she is silent.

❀

The girl wants to cry out for mother who is hurt and needs her help. She wants to scream. She wants to run but she is trapped. And so is brother.

The girl is standing in brother's mess, and when she lifts her foot, brother's mess drips from her toes, warm and wet. It has not gone down into the dirt and clay and disappeared forever. She does not understand.

The girl listens for mother. She is gone now. But mother will come back for them. She said so. After all the mad noises and sad noises and hurt noises, the girl heard mother say, Stay quiet, stay small, stay hidden. I'll be back for you.

The girl looks around for someplace safe to hide, someplace safe to wait. But inside this world of quiet things and soft things, safety is not found, and so she lies flat against the floor, the wood somehow colder than the earth.

❊

A pungent smell wakes Adelaide, and the ticking clock echoes from her bedroom, tapping vehemently against her skull. *Wake-wake-wake.* The room brightens with each passing second.

Adelaide sits upright on the sofa and struggles to piece together the events of the night before. Her calf throbs, and the wood floor spins beneath her. She closes her eyes until the nausea passes. The smell in her cabin is as piercing as the sound of her clock, and she brings her nightgown to her nose. Dirt, decay, fungus, and something that Adelaide cannot place.

A puddle of dark liquid seeps along a crease in the wood, disappearing beneath the sofa, and trickling closer and closer to the floorboard that pulls away from the nails. Adelaide snatches a pillow from the sofa and smothers the liquid before it can further penetrate her sanctuary. A quick sniff of the fabric confirms her suspicions. Urine.

Adelaide gasps. The children! They are nowhere in sight. Have they escaped? She stands, clutching the side table for support, nearly knocking it to the floor. She begins to call out for them before realizing she doesn't know what to say. They have no names, they share no language, and she has no more grass to throw.

The children are not under the bed. They are not behind the sofa, nor in her bedroom closet. Adelaide paces outside her cabin, peering into the trees, and inside the chicken coop. She walks along the river, but the children are not there either.

She doesn't want to look at the place where the chain still dangles over the wattle fence. But she must.

Adelaide listens to the morning air, but it betrays no secrets, and the spotlight of the rising sun leaves little room for doubt—the wild woman is gone.

Adelaide rushes from the corner of the fence and falls into the dirt. The shovel lies just beside the trap, tossed haphazardly, its blade shoved into a mound of dirt. The dirt is red.

An innocent woman has torn her own injured foot from these steel jaws because of Adelaide's sanctimonious actions. Her wonderful plan, isn't that just swell? Adelaide is an intelligent woman, but the best she could think of was, Let's kill the beast? Like a villager consumed by mass hysteria, she'd convinced herself that this was her only choice. And for what? A carrot? A pumpkin?

Adelaide doesn't deserve to live. She should have shoved those pills so deep down her gut, they'd have made it straight to hell before she did.

The wild woman is out there somewhere, injured, leaving blood in her wake like sweet candies for predators more dangerous than herself. And the children must be with her, traumatized, and traveling with a mother who is bleeding profusely. And who may or may not live to see the next sunrise.

Adelaide picks up the shovel and tunnels into the earth until blisters pop on her moist palms, distracting her from the pain in her calf. She shovels until her mind is so occupied with the growing hole that she is no longer thinking about the children she tried to kidnap. She digs until she can no longer remember the last few days, nor the reason for digging this hole in the first place. Ah, yes. To bury the trap. She should simply walk away, never think of it again. But the forest has a long memory, and if she does not bury it, her little homestead in the woods will become a place to be avoided. A cavity of sorrow and regret. Another floorboard that pulls away from the nails.

Avoidance is far from forgetting. But burying is a hell of a lot closer.

Adelaide has been a fool. She has no business raising children. That time for her is over now and everyone is better for it. She will continue with her life for a few more days, and she will not think of the children or the wild woman a moment longer. She will get her bearings, and then, when she is ready, she will feed Henry and the girls one final snack. She will straighten up her house, clear the garden. And then.

And then.

Then she will sleep.

Adelaide hobbles to the hole she has dug and drops the trap into its gaping mouth. The walls collapse immediately under its weight, and Adelaide need only kick a few lumps of dirt on top before she no longer sees the trap smothered in a feral woman's blood.

Freed from the steel in her arms, Adelaide already feels lighter. The sun rises beyond the trees, casting vibrant copper shadows across the landscape. Adelaide dusts her hands on her nightgown, which is now so dirty that it will likely become tomorrow's cleaning cloth, and walks toward her cabin.

There are still potatoes on her kitchen counter. Some may be rubbish, but some may yet make a decent breakfast for her. And as for chickens, well, chickens simply love rubbish.

The kitchen faucet spits to life and coughs cold, clean water into the sink. She pulls a small wooden bowl from the cupboard and begins to pare away the hardened outside of her potato slices. The chickens will be pleased.

Outside the window, Henry and the girls pluck at sluggish insects, and Adelaide raps on the window with her knuckle.

"I've a yummy breakfast comin' your way," she says, as if this morning were the same as any other. As if she hadn't maimed a woman last night and put an entire family at mortal risk. As if she doesn't have the urine of a petrified child staining her floor. As if she had never been so cruel and selfish.

Adelaide stops cutting and looks behind her. The feeling of being watched is overwhelming, and she squints through the morning haze. Her living room is empty. There is no one at her windows. But to be sure, Adelaide walks the length of her cabin before returning to the sink.

Once the final potato has been trimmed, she wipes the smears from her knife.

And then she sees motion captured in the reflection of the blade.

Adelaide spins, driving her back against the sink.

The children are right there—tucked above the large hutch in the corner of her kitchen. They huddle together, their eyes angry and accusatory. More than likely, they are simply scared, and Adelaide knows this, but her guilt leaves no doubt of their contempt.

Adelaide places the knife against the counter, and it topples from her grasp in a loud clatter, a reminder of how little control she currently has over her own body. Over anything.

The children jolt at the sound.

Adelaide forces herself to breathe.

"How . . ."

Her voice is quiet, barely a whisper, and she struggles to finish the sentence. How . . . are you still here? How . . . did you get up there? How . . . are you feeling?

Perhaps she should say, Welcome to my home. Perhaps she should say, I'm sorry.

But it doesn't matter what Adelaide says at all—they can't understand her anyway.

Adelaide pushes herself from the sink and the children recoil at her approach. She holds up her hands.

"It's okay. I'm not going to hurt you."

One of the children squeaks and buries his head against the wall, while the other continues to watch Adelaide. The children are clearly frightened. Wild. And likely hungry.

But they are not alone. They have Adelaide now.

Adelaide does not break eye contact for fear the children may leap on her back like feral monkeys, ripping at her hair and tearing at her eyes. The children are older than she originally thought. Her estimation is no doubt imprecise, but she suspects they are about five or six years old. Though petite, they are remarkably fit, their bodies a tight bundle of sinew, muscle, and hide. They are filthy, their hair matted and caked with mud.

They are stunning. Adelaide is breathless in the face of such beauty. They are like creatures from a storybook, or fine sculptures carved in stone.

Adelaide is as frightened as the children—perhaps more so—but she is also excited for this new adventure. She does not want to bring past failures into the present, but deep down, Adelaide has already begun to think, now I have someone to love again.

She approaches, a mere inch at a time, until she stands just below the children.

She raises her head and stares into the children's wide, pleading eyes. She smiles, almost laughs. They flinch.

"Nothing to fear, little ones. I'm as lost as you are."

❁

The girl pulls brother farther away from the woman with the wild eyes and from her long, scary hands reaching for them.

The woman looks a little like mother, but also not like mother at all. Her skin is different from mother's. And her lips are different from mother's. And there's something bright and soft covering her entire body, and that's the most different thing of all.

Brother jumps and squeaks every time the woman speaks, and the girl jumps, too, because the woman does not speak words, only sounds that aren't really words at all.

The woman's eyes are the color of the sky during the time of the flowers. The girl didn't know eyes could look like that. She wonders if one day her eyes will look like that, too. She hopes not. Those kind of eyes scare her.

The girl wants to scratch her leg and brush her hair from her face, but she can't move. Not with the woman looking at her with those eyes and making sounds that aren't words. Near the square forest inside the forest, where mother got hurt, the woman was happy and kind. But she's not throwing grass anymore. She's not fun anymore.

The girl looks up but there is no sun to help her see. She looks down but there is no mud to cover her body. She looks around but there are no trees to climb.

Brother claws at the girl's arm and she speaks to him softly and tells him it is okay, even though she's not sure it is okay. Because this is no forest, and there is nowhere to hide from a beast with eyes the color of the sky.

❀

9

Adelaide spends the afternoon trying to coax the children from the kitchen hutch, but no amount of pleading, cooing, or tempting with small bits of cooked potato make any progress.

It is only once she leaves the cabin for some fresh air, locking the door behind her, that the children relinquish their post.

When Adelaide returns from the river, she is filled with renewed determination, but as she steps inside, she notices the children are no longer in the kitchen. Adelaide shuts the door immediately as though they may scurry past her feet like shifty little mice. She begins to call out to the children but thinks better of it.

Adelaide knows they are here. She doesn't know *how* she knows, but she senses it—she is not alone in her cabin.

Adelaide steps on something small and sharp. A sunflower seed. The remaining sunflower heads have been pulled from their rope above the kitchen sink, and a small trail of dried leaves and debris traces a path across the living room. Highlighted in the last rays of the setting sun are little specks and kernels, leading directly under her bed. And there, barely visible in the shadows, the sole of a small foot, toes curling and wriggling. Adelaide can't help but smile.

She fills a bowl with water and walks into her bedroom. A floorboard groans under her weight, and the little foot disappears beneath the bed. Adelaide tucks the bowl just under the bed frame, and then sits on the edge of the mattress.

Inch by inch, she wedges herself farther onto the bed, and nestles her head between her pillows. She is quiet for a long while, listening to the ticking clock, and watching the familiar stains on her ceiling.

She hears the children resume their feast, the tiny crunches of sunflower seeds amplified in the stillness of the evening. She lies awake, listening to each bite, each nibble. The water bowl slides across the floor.

Shadows fill every corner of her home. Somewhere far away, tucked deep into the Blue Ridge Mountains, a coyote howls. Adelaide shudders and steals a glimpse at the darkening window. She wishes the children would climb into bed with her and allow her to pet their heads, wipe their faces, kiss their foreheads. She wants to comfort their fear, and also her own. But it is not the night for such things. There may never be a night for such things. But still, she can't stem the fantasy.

Adelaide should acclimate the children to her voice, even if they can't understand her words, and she decides to tell them a story. She tries to remember the fairy tales of her youth, of her daughter's youth. What was the one with the two children in the woods with the bread crumbs? Adelaide thinks it would be quite fitting, and she almost laughs. But then she remembers the part about the witch in the cabin, trying to cook the children in the oven, and thinks that perhaps she should recite something else. Ah yes, the boy who loses his parents in the wild and is raised by the monkeys and the tigers and the snakes. That's the one.

Adelaide clears her throat as quietly as possible and makes her voice small and soft.

"Once upon a time, deep in the woods . . ."

Adelaide wakes in the middle of the night to barking hounds and beams of light careening through her cabin. At first she is confused, and thinks it only a dream. But here it is again—a light so rigid, it is nearly steel. She covers her eyes to shield them from the onslaught. Dogs clamor at her window, and there are other noises as well—jostling feet and hushed whispers.

She thinks of the two young men at her door, mere days ago. And the old man, watching her cabin from the driveway.

We.

Adelaide bolts upright and lowers her feet to the floor. She mustn't wake the children; they'd be scared. Flashlight beams pour into her cabin, and she lunges for the curtains, wrestling them closed.

A silhouette appears at her bedroom window and taps a slow knock against the glass.

Adelaide looks around for something to grab, some kind of weapon. She thinks of the paring knife in the sink, and although every cell in her body screams at her to stay put and stay quiet, she bolts to the kitchen (hips go left to avoid the corner stool, footsteps wide to dodge the floorboard that pulls away from the nails).

Adelaide hopes she won't have to use it, but the knife feels good in her hand. She tiptoes back into her bedroom, toward the window, and the silhouette.

Adelaide whispers against the glass, "What do you want this time of night?"

His full voice answers her. "What time of night would that be?"

She must admit she does not know.

"Go away. Leave me alone."

"Our dogs are alertin' all over your property. We think you know what's goin' on in these woods."

"I don't." Her breath tides in and out of her lungs.

"I think you answered too fast, witch. You wanna try again?"

"I want you off my property. Now." Her voice cracks.

"Nothin' but God's property out here in the mountains."

Adelaide slumps against the wall and slides to the floor, pulling her knees to her chest. Who does she think she is? She is no mother bear, and these scared babies are not her cubs, no matter how much she wishes it so. How many men are circling her cabin right now? And what can she possibly do to protect these children—an old woman with a three-inch paring knife—against formidable men with flashlights and fists?

She feels like crying, but the tears won't come. And then she sees— nearly occluded by blankets and hidden by shadow, two small bodies beneath her bed. They are on all fours, their bodies still, their eyes trained upon the glass like the hunting dogs whining outside.

A *tap-tap-tap* on the glass.

"We ain't leavin' till we get answers. If there's no sleep for us, there's damn sure no sleep for you, witch."

"Stop calling me that."

"Witch don't like to be called witch," he calls over his shoulder. Another man laughs.

The children grunt, a sound of defiance. So they are brave little savages.

Shapes moves beyond the curtain. One of the men spits against the window, and the shadow of it trickles down the glass.

The children emerge from beneath the bed, shoulders tensed, eyes trained on the figures outside. They raise their faces to the window and begin to growl.

It is low at first, barely audible, but Adelaide hears. She is fascinated.

The children bend low to the floor, backs arched, feet readied behind them, as if preparing to rocket through the glass at any moment. The growls grow louder, merging into one collective sound of the earth.

The growl becomes a howl and the howl becomes a bark, and now the children are baying like goddamned coyotes, heads rising to the ceiling.

Picture frames rattle and the walls seem to sway. Every hair on Adelaide's body stands on end.

"What in the hell," a man says. "Wolves?"

"Ain't no wolf," answers another.

The men fall away from the window, their silhouettes blurring and quickly disappearing. The hounds follow.

The room spins around Adelaide. She may vomit. Faint. She could blame it on trepidation, or awe, but she knows in her gut and soul that it's because of the sound. A bizarre frequency strums the room, and her body has no defense against it. She struggles to stand. She fights to keep her eyes open, because the sight—oh, the glorious sight!—of these children transforming into beasts is the most beautiful thing she's seen in all her life.

Outside the window, men shout at one another, fear evident in their voices. Skidding footfalls. Slamming truck doors. Headlights illuminate the window and the screech of tires spinning against rock fills the empty spaces between howls as the men speed away.

The children bark a few more times before collapsing into each other and crawling back under the bed. They do not look back.

Adelaide is left alone on her bedroom floor. Two children less than five feet away, and yet she may as well be on a rock in the middle of the river. These children belong to no one but the forest, and she needs to release them. She knows this now. Adelaide brought the children into her home to protect *them*, not the other way around. They are wild animals, and she has jailed them. Tonight she will let them rest, but tomorrow she will set them free. Adelaide was wrong to take them in the first place. She was wrong to think they could be a family.

She stays on the floor a while longer and tries to re-create the sound in her mind. She wants to remember everything.

Adelaide ignores Henry as he scratches at her doorstep. She ignores the sound of Zelda and Moffit squabbling over a stray bug. She is too busy watching the shadows beneath her bed.

She awoke especially early this morning, unable to reconcile what would make her happy with what must be done. She paced, cleaned the outhouse, even walked along the riverside until a noise in the brush spooked her and sent her scampering to the cabin.

Adelaide now sits on the floor, her back to the door, watching, waiting, deciding. She appraises the bite wound on her calf, surprised to see no sign of a blossoming infection.

As soon as the children wake, she will prop open the cabin door, and then prepare breakfast. From the kitchen, she won't look back, won't steal even one more glimpse. And by the time her breakfast is ready, they will be gone. Everything will be over. Like it never even happened.

Adelaide closes her eyes and pushes her skull into the door, scolding herself for wishing everything to be meaningful. Life isn't eloquent. It's a big goddamned mess. There doesn't always need to be fanfare or pageantry. Sometimes you just have to open the door and turn your back. She's too old to be deluding herself with fantasies of family, and children, and togetherness, and knitted booties, and colorful drawings taped to her cabinets, and cuddles around the fireplace, and . . .

Adelaide forces herself to stop before she weeps, for she imagines she is too old for that, too.

A dirty little face peers out at her from beneath the bed. The little girl, she believes. They regard each other, and Adelaide tries to memorize the girl's eyes. Eyes that are much too insightful and clever for a person so young, and oddly familiar.

Adelaide taps her fingers on the floor in an effort to stay focused, and an echo comes from the bedroom as the little girl taps her fingers in response. Adelaide knows this game. She touches her nose. The little girl touches her nose. Adelaide pulls on her ear, and the little girl pulls on her ear. Adelaide wonders how far she can push the child. She taps a pattern on her face: nose-chin-nose. The little girl smiles and repeats on herself: nose-chin-nose.

Adelaide nods her head and smiles broadly. "Very good," she whispers. "One more time."

She holds up one finger to make sure the girl is paying attention. Forehead-cheek-nose-clap.

The little girl regards her sternly. Either Adelaide's just given a secret attack command, or this child has decided that Adelaide has finally lost her mind, which is not too distant a prospect.

The child crawls just outside of the bed frame and sits cross-legged on the floor. So Adelaide sits cross-legged as well. The little girl holds up one finger for a good long second—to make sure Adelaide is paying attention—and then repeats the pattern: forehead-cheek-nose-CLAP!

The noise jolts her brother from his slumber. He shrieks and inches behind his sister, sheltered by the bed. The little girl begins to laugh large belly laughs, clasping her hands to her mouth to stifle the sound.

Adelaide can't help herself, and she collapses into a giggle on the cabin floor. She knows that when she stands her spine will be sore, and she will likely have a headache, but right now, Adelaide does not care. She grins at the little girl who grins back. No expectations. No obligations. Just two girls playing a silly game.

Once the laughter has faded, and Adelaide is left with a feeling of contentment and a curious little girl, she lifts her hand into the air and gives a very simple wave, hello.

The little girl waves back.

Adelaide knows that the front door will remain locked today. And maybe tomorrow, too. Because Adelaide knows many more games.

PART 2
BEASTS

10

It took a few days, but the children have stopped sleeping beneath Adelaide's bed.

They now sleep under the living room table, which they've draped in blankets, sheets, and miscellaneous clothing—their own private tent. As if they are camping in the woods. Adelaide notes the irony.

She encouraged them to sleep beside her in the bed at first, to no avail. She then offered the sofa. But they either misunderstood her suggestion, or she misunderstood their needs—misunderstandings are becoming a large part of Adelaide's days—because the pile of blankets she folded neatly on the floor as a makeshift mattress, and the sweaters she couldn't manage to wrangle over their naked little bodies, were transformed into a tent by the following morning. Adelaide gives them that. No harm done.

This morning, Adelaide wakes early and surveys the kitchen cabinets. Feeding two additional mouths has been a strain on her already neglected resources. She had not anticipated she would have to endure another winter, and so did not stock her shelves over the summer and fall months, nor had she sent her supply list last season.

Adelaide cracks the door of her cupboard in search of a suitable breakfast. She spots a jar of pickled tomatoes and a handful of crackers, likely stale but still half-wrapped in plastic.

Thumps and scratches from the living room—the children are awake.

Adelaide peeks around the corner to find them sitting cross-legged before their tent, patiently waiting. This is the new routine. Adelaide presents something edible procured from the back corner of a cabinet. The children sniff it. Sometimes they eat, sometimes not. Sometimes they drape her furniture with the food, or stash it in cracks and crevices, and she must search each night for hidden remnants beneath the sofa and tucked inside cabinets before they turn rancid.

Adelaide would have thought it impossible, but she believes their bodies may be growing even smaller. She needs to go down to the river. It's been too long since she's fished. Her old fishing rod is in the storage shed and the river is only a short walk away, but Adelaide has been hesitant to leave the children alone for too long. She fears they will have disappeared upon her return, as if they never existed at all.

But she also fears bringing the children outside. Will they disappear into the forest without so much as a glance back to the woman who saved them from their savage life? Will they scamper away, searching for a mother who is likely dead by now? Cross paths with the men from the farm? She can't bear the thought. But Adelaide knows she will have to bring them outside sooner or later, if only to teach them to use the outhouse. She is tired of cleaning their mess from the floors.

Adelaide turns back to the jarred tomatoes. The lid is tight, and she struggles to find the right grip.

It's been hard to get a smile, or any emotion, from the children in days. Neither child allows her to get too close. They do not yet trust her, and Adelaide can't blame them. She wouldn't trust her either.

They stare at her as she struggles with the jar, expressionless, indifferent, as if letting her know that she is no savior. As if Adelaide needs reminding that she is bad at this.

The lid slides free, taking half a fingernail with it. Her brittle nail bed cracks straight to the cuticle, and blood blossoms beneath the fracture. Adelaide winces, cries out. She searches the countertop and shuffles through cupboards and drawers, looking for the hand towels. Bright red splatters mar her floor, and she turns toward the children to make sure they are not frightened.

They stare at her still—impassive, unmoving. Behind their stiff little heads, a pile of hand towels atop the makeshift tent.

❁

The girl watches the woman. Beside her, brother trembles. She senses his desire to investigate the shiny thing the woman is holding. She is curious, too. There is something in it the color of the bird that makes the *yeep* sound, like the food they ate with mother in the square-shaped forest just outside this place. Where mother screamed and bled the same color. The food was good. She remembers liking it. The girl touches brother's knee with her own. He grows still, and she knows he has understood.

They only have to wait and stay alive until mother comes. Brother has little patience. The girl is used to it. She will have to be mother until mother comes.

The woman fights with the shiny thing, and then she makes a loud noise.

The woman is hurt. The girl feels a pressure in her chest. She does not like it when people get hurt. It is like she is hurt, too.

The woman puts the shiny thing on the counter, and in the sunlight, it glows the color of the pointy flowers with the dark spots that make you sick. The girl remembers being very sick from eating those flowers. She remembers the forest going pale, and the leaves becoming fuzzy, and the sounds disappearing. She remembers being carried in mother's arms. There was a moon, and then another sun, and then another moon. That moon lasted a very long time before the sun came again, and the colors returned, and the noises came back. The girl never ate those flowers again.

The woman is searching for something, and she looks mad.

The woman looks right at them and the girl holds her breath. Blood drips onto the floor and she realizes that the woman is not mad, only hurt. The girl also realizes that the woman is looking for the soft squares they took from the food room last night. She doesn't want the woman to become mad, so she takes one of the soft squares from their sleep cave and stands. Brother looks at her, his eyes big. He shakes his head. But the girl has to be mother until mother comes. And mother would take care of the hurt woman because mother is kind.

The girl stands and nearly falls because her legs are tingly from sitting so long. She inches toward the food room. Standing this close to the woman's scary eyes makes her shiver, and she sits at the woman's feet so she is not so close to her eyes.

The blood on the floor is turning the color of the berries that are made up of bunches of smaller berries and her mouth waters. The girl is very, very hungry. But she will be patient. She lifts her arm into the air and holds the soft square until the woman takes it. Now the woman can clean off her blood and feel better.

The girl watches big-eyed brother in the big room. It is dark here, not like in the forest. And the air doesn't smell like trees or water or animals or anything the girl recognizes. And it certainly doesn't smell like mother.

The girl reaches up her hand and grasps the fingers of the woman. She hopes this shows the woman that she should be kind, and not mad.

✿

Adelaide looks down at the dirty little hand in her palm. The girl's skin is rough and cracked, not at all like the velvety skin of a child. She is shocked by the proximity of the girl. Adelaide has never been this close to either child, and she examines every tiny detail. Dark freckles pepper the girl's slim shoulders. Her hair is curly, forming loop-de-loops along her hairline before the mats take over and transform the soft, precious curls into dirty lumps.

Something small and silver—nearly invisible—moves through the girl's hair. Adelaide leans closer to the child. The nearer she gets, the more silver dots appear. Little meteor showers of insects zip this way and that. Hundreds of bugs, tunneling in and out of the tangles. All over the child's tiny body, small silver parasites now evident against her skin, among the freckles. They must be everywhere. In the cabin. On Adelaide's hand that the child now holds. Crawling all over her knuckles and burrowing into her flesh. Adelaide gasps and the child jumps, scurrying back to her brother. And in a moment as small as the silver insects, the magic of the exchange is gone.

It seems today will be a good day to take the children to the river for a bath. Bugs have a way of making a person resolute.

Adelaide opens the door to a pale but glorious sight—this morning, the forest has offered them all concealment. In the Blue Ridge Mountains, fog banks crest over the mountaintops like foam. They loom higher and higher, mountains of their own making, until the roiling waves can take no more, and they cascade into the canyon, swallowing trees and boulders, hungry and demanding, conceding to nothing. Piece by piece, trees disappear beneath wild, white tongues.

The children perk up when she opens the door wider, but they do not come closer. They perch at the edge of the living room rug, an invisible, yet tangible, barrier they hesitate to cross.

Adelaide approaches the girl first. When she extends her hand, the child takes it, but there is uncertainty in her face. The girl looks at the floor and bites her lip, and when Adelaide feels her pull away, she squeezes the girl's hand, gently, like a mother would. Like she did all those years ago.

"It's alright, little one. Water. Bath. Clean?"

The child does not understand, and Adelaide feels silly to have spoken as though she might. But the girl allows herself to be pulled from the rug.

The boy shakes his head vehemently. Something verbal is passed between the children, something Adelaide cannot translate. Vowels and consonants in no recognizable order. Adelaide extends her other hand to the boy, hoping he will take his sister's lead.

He does not.

But as they leave the safety of the cabin, Adelaide is glad to see him bounding down the steps to catch up with them after all. She offers a simple smile over her shoulder before turning back to the path.

The fog is still thick, but its hunger is satiated. It now pools at their feet, spinning in sleepy vortices as they walk. Fog has a way of drowning out sound, and today is no exception. The forest is silent.

Adelaide is grateful for the fog. She can barely see through the trees, which means the children can barely see through the trees. Maybe they won't run away from her today.

Mist clings to the river's surface, and Adelaide tests the temperature of the chilly water before stepping in farther.

She gestures for them to follow her into the river, but they remain on the bank like two statues, in all their bronze glory. It is then that Adelaide realizes she is still clothed, her housedress floating on the surface like a pale pink lily pad. She must look ridiculous to these children of the forest. She should undress but finds herself uncharacteristically shy. It would be inappropriate to expose them to her nakedness. There are decency standards when it comes to children. Societal standards. But what society? Adelaide looks to the children watching her, waiting to see what she will do. She is on the precipice of a breakthrough. She can feel it. Adelaide *must* be the one to lead. Leading cannot be left to children. They need her to be strong. Authoritative. They need her to be just a bit more *feral*.

And in that moment, her mind is made. Adelaide gathers the skirt of her dress and lifts it from her body, flinging it onto the rocks by the riverside.

Adelaide is no stranger to nakedness in this river, but with her two young spectators watching her every move, she suppresses the urge to cover herself, to turn away and stay protected beneath the waters. They don't want to see a shy old lady. They want to see a wild woman.

Adelaide stands proud in the waist-deep water as they examine her. How different she must look from their mother. Do they know that their mother, too, will look like this one day? Or that they will as well? Adelaide doubts they've seen another human being in their entire lives, other than their mother. They must know nothing of friends, cousins, grandparents. Of fathers. Something churns in Adelaide's mind. Those dark, bewitching eyes. The ones that still haunt her at night, even all these years later.

The children laugh, returning her focus to bath time, where it belongs.

Adelaide laughs as well. She jumps in and out of the water, her haphazard nakedness only making them laugh harder.

Adelaide puts on her best mean-but-still-smiling face, and she furrows her brows at the children. "Who do you think you're laughing at?"

The children are cackling now, collapsing to their knees and falling over each other.

Adelaide raises her shoulders until they are practically above her head and she stomps widely through the river as the children run in tight circles on the embankment.

Adelaide submerges her hands in the water and flings it at the children. They squeal with glee, twisting and leaping to avoid each icy drop.

Adelaide is delighted when the children rush to the river to join her, and utterly exhausted by the time they begin to slow.

This is the first time she and the children have had an opportunity to just be themselves, and Adelaide makes a mental note to bathe with them more often.

The little girl tugs on Adelaide's hand, pulling her toward the deeper part of the river. Adelaide follows, offering her a smile, and together they sit on the widest stones where Adelaide often sits to submerge herself.

She looks into the girl's eyes, and the child raises her eyebrows in response. If she knew what Adelaide was looking for, she would clench her eyes tightly shut and never open them again. But these worries are for grown-ups, not for children.

She shows the little girl how to take the sand and rub it into her skin, but it seems the girl has done this before, and she reaches into the river-bed, buffing sand and clay across her shoulders. She rubs it down her arms and across her stomach, pushing a kernel into her tiny belly button. When Adelaide brings sand to the girl's hair, the girl flinches and backs away, as if she's never known hair can become clean, too. Adelaide demonstrates on her own messy hair. She rubs the muck into her scalp and pulls it down the length of her mane. She brings it in front of her forehead and twists it into a giant silver horn. She finds her best goblin face and growls (politely) at the little girl, who laughs wildly. Laughter comes easily to the very young. She envies them.

The little boy follows, coating his skin in clay and sand, buffing away all the dirt and bugs that have claimed his body.

The little girl sits before Adelaide, and she burrows her fingers into the girl's scalp, coating her hair with clay, scraping away layer upon layer of sweat and dead skin cells and dirt and insects. Some of the hair loosens, but full release is likely many baths away.

After a rinse, the children float on their backs, speaking of things Adelaide will never understand. Even if she wanted to ask, she wouldn't know how. This is just the way it is, she imagines. But they've done pretty well so far without words. Maybe words are overrated.

Adelaide relaxes against a large stone, watching the fog through the foliage. The haze hovers just above the ground, clinging to trees, wrapping their gnarled trunks with wisps of gauzy cotton.

A dark shape rushes through the fog and Adelaide sits up, tight and erect. She tries to locate the shadow, but it has already disappeared. It was large, lumbering on all fours. No sound.

The figure appears again in her periphery. Darker this time. Closer, but still obscured. A whine pierces the fog, raining down all around them. The children rush from the river, their faces twisting to the left and to the right. Behind, above. They don't know where to look, and quite frankly, neither does Adelaide. But she knows she wants them all in the cabin. Now. Before she loses everything.

The wild woman, it seems, is still alive.

Adelaide grabs the children by their hands and runs, dragging them behind her as they wail, heads whipping from side to side, seeking the source of the sound.

The cabin feels so far away, like none of her footsteps are closing the gap. With visibility this low, she feels terribly outnumbered. Like the sky is in on it. Like the ground and the trees and the sun itself are all in on it. The forest, once again, has sent her a thief.

Adelaide tumbles through the front door, flinging the children into the living room, where they collapse onto their sleeping tent, sending the table and blankets spinning across the floor. She locks the door. Deadbolts it. Looks around for something to grab but sees only the children. And so Adelaide grabs them both, covers them with her body, and wraps her arms tightly around them as the pounding begins. The first assault comes from the door, the second from the kitchen window. Adelaide throws a blanket over them all, hiding under the bedsheets from the boogeyman.

From a wild woman.

The children are hers now. Out there, they were uncivilized, filthy, and covered in bugs. In here, they are clean and happy enough. They will flourish. They can finally be *children*. The creature she trapped in her garden is, admittedly, no mountain lion, but neither is she a mother, and Adelaide can do better.

The wild woman pummels the walls and the sound echoes through the cabin, unyielding, as though it will never end.

Until suddenly, it does.

Adelaide is too scared to look outside the blanket, so she holds the children beneath her, rocking them, hushing them, though they are already silent.

✿

Mother came for them, just like she said she would, but mother is still hurt. Normally, mother is very strong and very fast, but she was not very strong or very fast today, so the woman stole them again.

The air outside was thick and pale, and the girl couldn't see mother, not really. But she could feel her, and she could hear her.

Run, mother said. Run away.

But the woman's hands were so strong, and even though she and brother tried to run away, they weren't as strong as the woman. They will have to wait until mother is strong and fast again.

Unless they can find a way out on their own.

Tonight, the girl stands at the window with brother, and together, they push and pry and smell and lick the glass. The girl does not understand. She can see through it, like water, but she cannot taste it, like water. Or step through it, like water. Brother begins to cry until the girl shushes him.

Don't wake the woman, she says, and brother stops.

Perhaps there is a different way. The girl tiptoes to the door and jiggles the shiny thing that the woman uses to go outside. It only makes a little noise—not a big noise—but the girl waits until she hears the woman's sleep-breathing before jiggling it again.

The girl runs her hands over the door, which looks a little like a tree. It smells a little like a tree, too, if she gets really close and presses her nose against it. But it is not a tree. It is a pretend tree. Like the small birds that make the sound of the really big birds, even though they are not the really big birds. The woman is pretending, too. She pretends that she is their mother.

After licking the window and sniffing the door, the girl grows tired. She curls up with brother in their sleep cave in the big, dark room. The girl touches brother's hair. It is soft as a feather now, and a little wet. Brother leans forward and touches his forehead to the girl's forehead, and then falls asleep.

Instead of the moon and the stars, the girl stares at the soft, swaying sky of their sleep cave. On it are little pictures of the flower with the sharp thorns. They are all around them, and though they are pretty to look at, the girl doesn't know how anyone can sleep surrounded by thorns.

✿

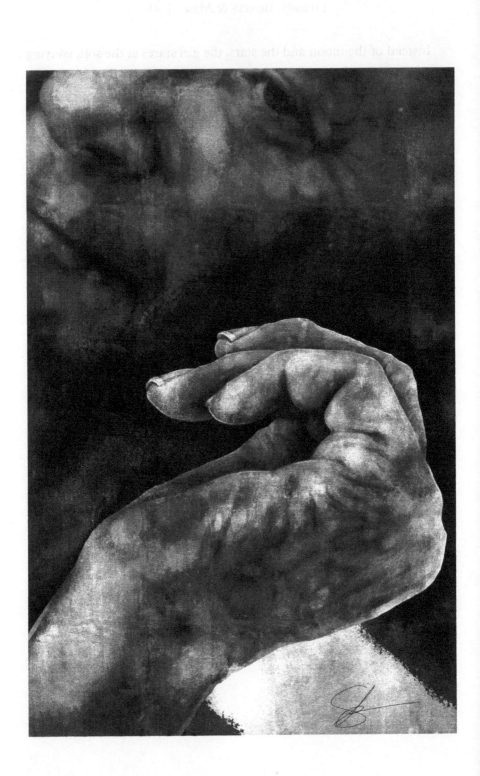

11

In the morning, Adelaide sits on the sofa, working a comb through the girl's hair. Yesterday's bath has loosened the mound, and the comb is finally finding some relief. As Adelaide works, the boy lifts the rug to peer beneath it. He dangles his fingers before the fireplace to see how close he can get to the flames. He smells the sofa and fingers the weave of a basket.

"You're a curious one, you are. Like a little bird, hopping from tree to tree," she says to him. The boy does not acknowledge her words.

As Adelaide lay in bed last night, scarcely a hint of sleep, all she could think was, *I* must *take better care of the children.* They aren't pets. They need guidance and protection. Interaction. And this is something Adelaide is willing to do, every waking hour for the rest of her life. She shudders to think she nearly killed herself a couple of weeks ago, never knowing these children existed, trapped in a life of hardship, at the mercy of the elements. They are lucky she has rescued them.

Last night was quiet. No beasts. No men. She tries to convince her-self that she was wrong, and that the thing chasing them through the fog was simply a bear, and not the wild woman. Somehow this is more com-forting than the alternative. Adelaide can handle a bear.

Adelaide works loose a knot of the girl's hair and coils it around her finger. The children appear healthier now. And more content. One should never underestimate the power of a good bath.

"You have lovely hair, little one. We'll have to try a ponytail soon. Do you know what a ponytail is? I suppose not."

Adelaide is well versed in one-sided conversations. Her chickens will offer a cluck or chortle every now and again. The children offer a grunt.

"Of course, we will have to find something to tie it up with. Don't lean on your elbows. There you are. Sit up like a proper little girl." Adelaide wrangles the girl's body into a better position and resumes the grooming. "And we will have to give you a name soon, before your name officially becomes 'little girl,' what do you think about that? Yes, and your brother, too."

Another curl falls free.

Adelaide had expected the detangling to take days, but after a few short hours in front of the fireplace, the girl's mane is nearly liberated.

"We have pets, you know," Adelaide continues. "Chickens, in fact. They don't lay eggs anymore, but it's no bother to keep them around. They keep the bugs down and eat the table scraps. They're good chick-ens. You'll meet them soon."

The girl pokes at a curl dangling before her eyes. It's possible she's never seen one before, considering the state of her hair. She pulls it taut and releases, watching it spring back into formation. Her body jumps a little and Adelaide assumes it was a laugh. The girl sits straighter and pushes her head farther into Adelaide's lap.

The little boy examines a sofa pillow, stands on the tips of his toes to see how tall he is against the wall, and runs to the window to look out-side. The little girl watches all of this, never moving, never speaking. But then a sudden clip of noise escapes the girl's lips, and Adelaide stops grooming to watch the boy's response. He sits before his sister, and the girl begins to comb his tangles with her fingers. He is quiet and motionless. So that's what that sound means. Adelaide tries to commit it to memory, but the vowel and consonant sound has already left her mind as if she never heard it at all.

She places her whole hand on the little girl's head and grins. "So, we've got a little bird and a caretaker," she says.

The children offer nothing in the way of a response. The girl continues to groom her brother's hair with her fingers, with a less transformative effect than Adelaide's comb.

"Yes. Little Bird. I like that," she says as she works loose another lock of hair.

Flakes of dried river clay rain down on Adelaide's knees, and she thinks of the forest. She considers the trees and the fog and the mountains that surround her. And the river, which provides water, food, cleanliness. She thinks of her secret spot beneath the maple tree—her favorite little corner of the Blue Ridge Mountains.

"Rivers are a source of strength, you know. Commanding at times. Gentle at times." Adelaide gently grasps the girl's shoulders. "Just like you."

The girl peers up at Adelaide with eyes brown as a lump of wet clay straight from the depths.

River. Wonderful.

Before long, River's hair is unbound, curls drifting through the air as if no longer bound by gravity.

"You are done, little one!"

The girl looks up at her and then motions to her brother. Adelaide nods, and as if there is no language barrier at all, the children swap places and Adelaide begins to comb Little Bird's hair.

River sits against the wall and listens as Adelaide speaks of turning leaves, and of the few birds that will remain over winter, and of the goats she had once. Neither child responds, but they grunt as though acknowledging her words. It's nice to have someone to talk to.

When Little Bird's curls flow freely, Adelaide is excited to show them. She stands to retrieve the small, round mirror by the front door, and sits on the sofa, motioning for the children to join her.

They approach cautiously, and Little Bird is the first to brave a look at his reflection.

Little Bird is riveted. His eyes bulge, his mouth gapes, and he pushes his face closer to the mirror until his nose bangs the glass. He clutches his face and looks to Adelaide as if she meant him harm.

Adelaide smiles. "It's alright, child. It's a mirror."

Little Bird rubs the tip of his nose and inches closer. He touches his chin and chirps when his reflection does the same. He opens his mouth and laughs at his teeth and tongue.

Adelaide motions for River to join them.

River smiles and bounds toward them on her knees, eager to see what her brother has discovered. As Little Bird collapses into giggles, River leans forward to peer into the mirror.

Adelaide is not prepared for the girl's reaction. River squawks and drops to the floor, fear transforming her beautiful face into something brutal and untamed. She bares her teeth and claws her fingers into the floor as she scoots away from Adelaide and the mirror. The girl kicks her feet, and the mirror is airborne. It spins across the room, catching the sunlight as it descends, illuminating the walls with sharp flashes of light.

The mirror lands with a blast, fragments careening through the cabin. Adelaide shields her face, but the children know nothing of breaking glass. Specks of blood bloom on the children's bellies, arms, cheeks. They look to Adelaide, mute, the quiet like a silent alarm, charged and ready.

"Oh, little ones," Adelaide cries, rushing to them on the floor, and carefully plucking chunks of glass from their skin.

Adelaide's knees are cut and bleeding, but she will tend to that later. She hurries to the kitchen and returns with a dampened washcloth. The children allow her to lift them from the floor, one by one, and place them on the sofa. Adelaide wipes the blood away, tending to each nick and scrape.

The children will be alright. Nothing has cut too deeply. But they are now motionless and uncertain—all smiles, grunts, and other communications gone silent.

When Adelaide finishes, she collapses into the cushions. How stupid of her. How ignorant. The image replays over and over in her mind. The spinning mirror, their looks of terror. She'd covered her own face instead of shielding the children. She has forgotten the role of a mother, wrapped up in this place and in herself for so many years. She's forgotten the responsibility, the selflessness. Or, Adelaide worries, perhaps she's never known. Perhaps that is the most significant truth of all.

River pulls the washcloth, stained with swatches of red and pink, from Adelaide's lap. She does not look up as she leans forward and gently dabs the blood on Adelaide's knees.

Daytime with the children is optimistic, full of hope and breakthroughs and newfound trust. But at night, second guesses, fear, and frustration knock an endless percussion on Adelaide's skull.

She stares at the stains on her ceiling, blooming larger than ever thanks to the fall rains, and she listens to the silence of the children. The lack of sound is palpable and stifling in the darkness. They are asleep beneath their makeshift tent and Adelaide resists the urge to check on them one more time. The ticking clock sounds like breaking glass—snap-snap-snap—and Adelaide can lie in bed no longer.

She stands and walks to the kitchen, peering through the window and into the night.

The trees are a harsh blue. Wispy branches, torn and tangled by the wind, reach to the sky as if in prayer. And the sound. The sound is there, too. It returns every night lately, and Adelaide has come to know it well. The mangled howl from human vocal cords. Sorrowful and yearning. The wild woman, grieving the loss of her children. She is not close this night, but neither is she far. Adelaide can't see her—nighttime is too dense for an old woman's sight—but she can hear her. Snapping branches as the woman gallops, and her sharp guttural declarations of heartache.

Adelaide swallows the knot in her throat and tries once more for sleep.

Outside her bedroom window, the wind whorls and bellows. Adelaide peeks outside to see if her chickens would like to come inside and keep her company, but they are not waiting outside her bedroom window tonight.

Adelaide plaits her hands against her chest and stares once again at the stains on her ceiling as she waits for sunrise.

A noise—soft but insistent. A touch.

Adelaide opens her eyes expecting daylight but is met with the violet glow of a morning too premature to call dawn. She doesn't remember falling asleep.

A shadow moves in her room, small and slow. Adelaide pulls the bedcover from her cheeks as her eyes adjust to the gloom.

Syllables. Vowels. A chirp.

She buffs the sleep from her eyes. "Good morning," she croaks to the children standing in her doorway, but neither child moves toward her. She offers them an outstretched arm, but they simply stare at Adelaide in silence. This is new.

"What is it, little ones?" she says to them as she shifts her legs over the side of the bed. "It's quite early, you know."

Adelaide stretches her arms, her neck, her fingers. She wonders if the children hear their mother rustling through the forest at night. Did they hear her last night? Is that what has woken them so early this morning? Oh, how she wishes she could speak to them.

Their spiraling redwood hair reaches halfway down their backs. Their stance is the same. Their voices, even devoid of human words, are like sounds from the same person. If it weren't for the display of a little penis now and again, Adelaide would never be able to tell them apart.

She wonders if she should try introducing clothing again. Soon, she thinks. But not today.

Adelaide envies the children, in a way. As if by being spared from the rest of the world, they are evolving into something closer to human than most of us will ever know. Something genuine and primal. These children have never had to escape the urban landscape, consumerism, industry, as she did. They were born free, and Adelaide aches to know what that is like. Perhaps they can teach her.

Adelaide doesn't know how to interpret all the things that flow through her mind, but she does know one thing for sure: it's time for some honest-to-goodness breakfast. She walks toward the children and pats their heads as she passes. They allow it.

In the kitchen, Adelaide peers out the window. The morning air breaks with streaks of golden light, illuminating her chickens just out-side the garden. Zelda and Moffit chase their morning feast, while Henry reserves his chase for only the meatiest of insects. Adelaide smiles. She should introduce the children to Henry and the girls today. They could all use a pick-me-up.

Adelaide opens her cabinets hoping for some canned garden rem-nants, perhaps some grains to fashion into oatmeal, but it seems the day has finally come when three mouths to feed are two too many. She could search the garden once more. There was nothing salvageable the last time she looked, but she may have missed something.

The fishing pole is in the shed, and the river still runs, which means fish still swim. She takes a deep breath, and the weight on her shoulders lightens. Adelaide turns to the children and clasps her hands together. "River, Little Bird, today we shall catch a fish for breakfast. How does that sound?"

The children bound across the kitchen, roused by her excitement.

"Okay," she says, marching to her bedroom and slipping into her housecoat and boots. The frost on her windows doesn't lie. It is cold today.

Adelaide reaches into her closet for sweaters for the children, and sees the inevitable struggle in her mind: River biting at the fabric, all barks and growls and whoops and chirps, as Adelaide yanks her arm through a sleeve; Little Bird wrapping pants around his neck, the deflated legs trailing behind him as he runs in circles; River dropping to the floor, kicking her feet at Adelaide, her pretty little forehead creased with insult.

No. This morning Adelaide does not have the resolve to win that battle. She whisks a blanket from their sleeping tent and glides it through the air like the sail of a ship, bundling the children into a pocket of cotton. They squeal and giggle and bounce on their feet.

"C'mon, you two. I just might need your help."

The children have developed a dependable habit of staying close to Adelaide on their treks to use the outhouse, waddling just behind her, side by side. They are more themselves in the fresh air. Eyes bright, ears perked, necks quick to turn toward any sound in the brush. But she keeps a close eye on them nonetheless, just in case today turns out to be the day they run away from her forever.

The fishing pole is easy to pluck from the other equipment. It is rusted, but it's never let her down, brittle though it may be. She turns to show the children, but they are gone.

Adelaide drops the pole. It can't happen. Not yet. She's not ready to lose them.

She scans the foliage, but there is no movement, no shadows, no sign of anything. She tries to call to them, but her words catch in her throat. If the children want to leave her, she is powerless to stop them.

Adelaide takes a deep breath and concentrates on the sounds of the morning: birds chirping, branches rustling in the wind, lizards in the fallen leaves. The lilting conversation of chickens. And a hushed whisper of syllables. The children! She follows the sound, rushing toward the back of her cabin, and when she finally sees them, Adelaide nearly collapses with joy.

River and Little Bird are on the ground, watching the chickens. Adelaide laughs. They huddle quietly beside each other, beneath their blanket. Motionless. She approaches, expecting the sound of her footsteps to disrupt their concentration. It does not. As she creeps closer, River holds out a flat palm as if to say, *Stop*.

Adelaide leans down to look at the children's faces and she takes a step back. They watch the chickens with rigid gazes. Their knees are bent and ready. Their teeth are bared.

"Oh my god!" Adelaide screams, and the chickens scurry off as the children recoil.

Adelaide can hardly believe it. The children were hunting Henry and the girls.

Adelaide bends down to their height. "No!" she says. "We do not hurt the chickens. They are pets." She makes a motion as if stroking a small animal with her hands. "Friends." She puts her arm around an imaginary person. And then Adelaide is out of hand gestures.

She snatches their hands and leads them straight to the river so they can fish, a more appropriate activity for two hungry children.

12

Before long, the first flurries of the season whiten Adelaide's window.

How long, this time, until her daughter brings provisions? A week? A month? The river will soon freeze over, and there won't be fish for months. Her daughter can be so heartless sometimes.

Adelaide lies in bed longer than she should, watching the glass bloom with fractal patterns. She is not yet ready to rise, to think. She is not yet ready for anything.

Last night, the wild woman was silent for the first time in weeks, and Adelaide had a peaceful night's sleep. No sorrowful baying. Just the blissful reticence of winter in the Blue Ridge Mountains.

A few nights ago, Adelaide awoke to a new sound. Closer than the wild woman, a much smaller cry: Little Bird, calling out to his mother from inside the cabin. It went on for an entire minute, longer than any minute Adelaide had ever known. His voice, like tin foil, like ice. Barely there, yet almost too much for Adelaide to bear. Adelaide did not know what to do, or if she should do anything at all. But then River spoke to him in their special-speak. Low, rushed. And Little Bird fell silent. That was a hard night.

And yesterday, another hard day. The water was too cold to bathe, and for the first time since the children's arrival, there was not a fish in sight. Nothing in the woods to forage, nor among the remnants of her garden. Yesterday, they went hungry. Adelaide tries to convince herself that hunger—and hunger alone—is to blame for the children's growing melancholy.

Becoming a mother again, the idea once romantic, has turned to panic in Adelaide's heart. It was hard enough the first time, when she was young and resourceful and ambitious. The children are safe in her cabin. They have a warm place to sleep, and she has the best intentions, of course. But what she doesn't have today is food. The children still refuse clothes, and they continue to watch the windows. Waiting. Hoping, perhaps, for liberation.

Adelaide listens to the clock. She counts the seconds, trying to convince herself to face the day. One . . . two . . . three . . .

The clock ticks, *now-now-now*.

Outside her window, Henry squawks an unhappy greeting to the sun. Perhaps he's awoken to find the insects are hibernating as well. Winter has come for them all.

Adelaide pulls herself upright and walks to the kitchen. There is no food to be found, but the trek is a deep-rooted habit, impossible to amend. Her stomach growls in a place so deep that her hips rattle. Today, she will come up with a solution. Today *has* to be that day. Adelaide grabs her housecoat to make her morning trip to the outhouse. The door squeaks, as it always has, but the two pairs of feet sticking out from the tent in her living room do not move. Adelaide steps quickly outside and shuts the door behind her.

The flurries have slowed in their descent, but the haze obscuring the sun indicates they will fall for a long while today. Adelaide stands just under the eave of her home as snowflakes dance before her eyes, gyrating and spinning onto her cheeks, her neck, her exposed shins. She breathes in the metallic coldness, and though her bones ache and her stomach rumbles, it is glorious. Adelaide, it seems, is grateful for another winter after all.

Adelaide circles her cabin and makes her way to the chicken coop. Henry complains loudly—he is not a winter chicken. Zelda scratches through the dusting of snow, upending sticks and clumps of dirt in the hope of finding a succulent squirming *something*. Adelaide looks for Moffit, but she is not outside with the others. Adelaide finds her inside the coop, feathers aloft, body shivering. When Moffit sees her, she careens onto the steps, whirling across the ground in a cyclone of copper feathers.

"Oh my, what a greeting."

Adelaide bends down to find the chicken still quaking. A single brown feather floats to the earth with the flurries. Moffit's eyes are dispirited, and she leans her weight into Adelaide's warm palm.

"I know how you feel," she says.

Moffit offers no response.

Adelaide gives Moffit one last scratch and then stands to watch Henry and Zelda march across the landscape of her property. Zelda is perfectly content with the change of season, preening her feathers and prancing on her tall legs through the snow. She and Henry battle over an unearthed beetle, and Adelaide waits to see who will emerge the victor. Zelda snatches a black, crooked leg and darts into the garden to devour her prize. Henry does not pursue. Adelaide smiles and walks toward her cabin. Back to River and Little Bird. Back to her new life.

The door handle is an ice cube in Adelaide's hand, but her cabin is pleasant, the embers in the fireplace still soaking her home with radiant warmth.

Something feels different. It's too quiet. Not a sleeping-child kind of quiet, but a trouble-brewing kind of quiet. Adelaide peeks into the tent. No twitching feet, no snoozing children. The cabinets are open in the kitchen. Drawers ajar. Bowls askew. The children have been busy in her absence.

"River? Little Bird?"

There is no response, not even a grunt or a squeak. Adelaide can see directly into her bedroom from the front door, but the children are not there either.

The floorboards creak beneath her weight as she circles behind the sofa. And then she sees it.

"Oh my god."

Torn pieces of paper. Handwritten words. Crayon drawings.

"No, no."

White yarn, arcing in impossible angles from years spent in small, tight loops.

Bent board. Crooked, rusted nails.

Adelaide gasps. The children have discovered the box under the floorboard that pulls away from the nails.

"What have you done!" she hollers.

The children shriek, shuffling away from the sofa.

Adelaide falls to her knees above the mess. Letters, torn and chewed. White and pink yarn disassembled and dispersed. Nine months of knitting, time, promise, love, hope. Gone. A smell of rot and dust hovers like a cloud above the gaping hole in Adelaide's floor. Things she hasn't looked at in decades—*couldn't* look at for decades—tarnished in the full light of the morning. Adelaide's hands tremble as she picks up torn pieces of paper from months of journal entries. She reads the writing, not even recognizing it as her own.

—my mind won't change. You are mine and—

—as safe a place as I can make it. We will be—

—hope you never know the kind of sorrow that—

— bad day, but today you kicked for the first—

The scraps drift from Adelaide's hands like falling leaves. She lifts the tangled mass of the receiving blanket and holds it to her face, breathing deeply, trying to hold it all within her lungs, as the box beneath the floorboard has held it all these years. There is a scent she recognizes, buried deep beneath the odor of moisture and time. For just a moment she is twenty years old again, eyes bright and expectant, stomach taut and teeming with life. Her young heart holds pain—raw and recent pain—but is still naive enough to be hopeful. A baby girl in her arms. Plump, shiny, pink, and crying. Wonderful delicious crying. Adelaide, a new mother. Tears and laughter. Alone, but also not. A new, small, perfect family.

And then it is gone, the scent dissipating into the air, which is growing colder by the minute. Adelaide lashes out, tugging furiously at the yarn in her hands. It tangles around her fingers, but she does not stop until the remainder of the blanket is fully undone. Only when it resembles nothing more than a pile of pink and white string can she hold back the tears no longer.

Adelaide spends the rest of the afternoon in bed, stomach empty, mind numb. She does not know where the children are, or what they are doing. Today, she does not care. Her mind drifts from memory to memory, thin slices of a life coming and going, lingering for only a moment before they are replaced by another.

Adelaide remembers her orange tent—the one she brought with her to begin her life in the Blue Ridge Mountains. How naive she was. A rip in the upper right corner. The black zipper with the paint chipped, silver flashing from beneath. She remembers the day she found this cabin, abandoned, neglected, and the day she gathered willow branches to build a garden. She remembers her goats, remembers hunting for rabbit and squirrel, her first chickens and that first scrambled egg cooked over the fireplace.

And she remembers the man, though she doesn't want to, never wants to. His stench, his grip, is never far from recollection, even all these years later. He is the old man from the farm; she knows this now. Adelaide had assumed he was a drifter, or a lost hiker. She believed he went far, far away after leaving her cabin that day. After she invited him in for a glass of water. After he left her bloodied and raw, an empty husk of a woman strewn across her own floor, his refuse taking root in her gut. To think of him this way—so close to her all these years—seems like a betrayal. As if he owed her his absence after what he did. As if he broke an unspoken agreement.

Maybe she is too anchored in her past. She knows her life's story well, all of its twists and turns as familiar as the scars and age spots on her skin. This new life? She knows nothing. Adelaide doesn't know what the next hour holds, let alone the next week. This is a foreign country, with its own societal boundaries and exotic languages.

Two pairs of feet pad into her bedroom, and she knows the children are standing beside her. She forces herself to turn toward them.

Little Bird is closest to her. In his arms, the small gray stuffed elephant from the box. He offers the toy to Adelaide. The fur is threadbare, the beaded eyes still black and shiny. She pushes his hand toward his chest, relegating the elephant to where it belongs. It is no longer hers. He hugs the stuffed animal, burying his face within it, rocking from side to side. River holds the small knitted cap, butter-yellow, cradled against her chest like a swaddled baby.

Adelaide sits up in her bed and smooths the covers around her lap. She offers her hand to River.

"Come here, little one," she says, her voice gentle. "We're going to be alright. I promise."

To Adelaide's astonishment, the girl climbs onto the bed and curls up in her lap.

She strokes River's hair and River strokes the knitted cap. Little Bird sits on the floor by the bed, content to cuddle his elephant all on his own while Adelaide comforts his sister.

River pokes her fingers in and out of the stitches. A thoughtless motion, but Adelaide smiles to see it treasured once again.

"Here, let me show you," she says, taking it from the girl's hands. "It's a hat. And it goes here."

Adelaide tugs the knitted cap over River's thick hair, stretching it until it covers her ears. River laughs, running her hands over her head.

The girl looks up and extends a tiny finger to Adelaide's forehead, tracing the lines that run across.

"What a surprise today has been."

And though she does not understand the words, River smiles. She brings her other hand to Adelaide's face and cups her temples. Adelaide isn't sure what the girl is doing until River pulls herself to her knees and dips her head forward to touch Adelaide's.

Any remaining words on Adelaide's tongue fall away. Words are meaningless anyway. She knows that now. And she requires nothing more.

Because Adelaide has just received a wild woman kiss.

❧

The girl holds the woman's head between her hands. Her fingers shake and she wonders if the woman can feel it. When she touches her head to the woman's head, the girl feels sad. But she feels other things, too—things she's felt before, but also things that she hasn't.

The woman is not mother, but sometimes she feels like a mother, and the girl misses being held and being loved, so she lets go of the woman's head and curls up in her lap. The woman is warm and soft, not hard like mother. But she is kind like mother, and even though she has strange eyes the color of the sky, the girl is not scared of them anymore.

The woman has given her a name. And brother, too. But she cannot say it. She has tried. They both have, late at night while curled up in their sleep cave, after the woman is asleep. Brother can almost say his name. His mouth makes funny shapes when he tries, but he's getting better. The girl will keep trying. She thinks maybe that would make the woman happy.

Brother curls up on the floor with the animal that is not real. His breathing slows and the girl thinks that maybe he is asleep now, and she relaxes against the woman's chest and begins to think.

Mother has not left them—she and brother hear her at night. Mother is still hurt. The girl can tell by her voice, and that makes her hurt, too.

Brother wants to run away when they are outside, but the girl tells him no. There is something in her head that tells her to stay with this woman for a little bit longer. This woman is hurt. She does not bleed, and she is not sick, but she is hurt somewhere deep inside. Mother would take care of someone if they were hurt. Brother doesn't understand, but he listens.

It is the time of the pale rain. The girl likes this time of year. It is quiet. Mother likes this time of year, too, and that makes the girl happy. They are always a little bit hungry during the time of the pale rain, but mother knows how to find the plants with the dark curly leaves that stick out from the ground. And buried under the plant that no longer has the fuzzy flowers are the fat creamy roots shaped like fingers. But the woman must not know about the fat creamy roots shaped like fingers, because they are still hungry.

Even though the woman doesn't know about the creamy roots, she keeps animals that are food. Right outside are the round birds that don't fly. But the woman doesn't eat the birds and won't let the girl and brother eat the birds either.

Mother says that if you don't eat for many days and many nights that you can die. And that means you go away forever. The girl wonders if there are different kinds of dying, because she's only seen animals die, and it can't be the same thing.

The girl wonders if she and brother will die. She wonders how many days and nights of being hungry make you go away forever.

❁

13

Adelaide wakes the next morning, surprised at how many hours she has slept. She is even more surprised to find River and Little Bird asleep in her bed. She hesitates to move for fear of waking them and breaking the spell, as if this were merely a mirage, a trick of her hopeful mind.

Adelaide is hungry, but the cabin is barren.

She wasn't supposed to be here, but she is, and so are the children, and as much as Adelaide would like to stay in bed all morning, admiring her new family, there is something she must do. And she should do it soon, while she's still half asleep.

Before she changes her mind.

They've gone a full day without food. Her shelves are empty, the forest is desolate, the river is frozen, and Adelaide doesn't know when her daughter will arrive with supplies. Or if she will arrive at all.

Adelaide opens a kitchen drawer and withdraws a knife as though she is simply preparing to slice some vegetables. Her hands tremble as she takes a washcloth from the hook and folds it into a square beside the cutting board. Sunlight floods through the small window, warming her skin, but she can't bring herself to look outside. Not this morning. Her stomach lurches, and bile fills her throat.

There is no food, no vegetables, no fish.

But there are chickens.

Adelaide slips into her coat and steadies herself against the door. Her hand lingers on the knob, but she forces herself to turn it and step into the snow.

There is nothing left to do. She has nothing else to give them.

Adelaide flexes her fingers as she stomps across the icy ground. She is a farmer—*a farmer, goddammit*—and this is what farmers do. The girls stopped laying years ago, and she should never have kept the rooster. Roosters are for meat. Hens are for eggs, then meat. That's it. Soil is tilled. Vegetables are grown. Chickens are meat. *Meat.*

She's done this before. Dozens of times. No different now. Adelaide pictures the steps in her mind. Scald, defeather, remove feet and head, discard innards, debone the meat, grease the skillet. Her mouth should be watering, but it's not.

All is serene on her land this morning, a stark contrast to her heart.

"Henry," she calls out, but feels guilty using their names. "Chickens!"

At the sound of her voice, Henry and Zelda practically fall down the ladder and tumble onto the ground. Moffit emerges behind, slower than the others.

Adelaide walks to the pile of firewood and sits on one of the stumps. The chickens careen toward her, likely hoping for sunflower seeds, but she is all out of treats these days.

Adelaide takes a deep breath and watches Henry and Zelda chase a few small insects, displaced from the woodpile. Moffit sits by Adelaide's feet, and she bends down to pet the bird. Moffit shivers and Adelaide picks her up, placing her on her lap. She expects the chicken to flutter down, but she does not.

"You know, we have children to think of now," Adelaide says. "It's not just about us anymore."

Henry looks up at her, his plum feathers swirling above his head like a halo. He looks as though he is waiting to hear more, so she continues. "We've had a good run."

Zelda joins the discussion, shaking her head and scratching her neck. A single feather floats through the air.

"This isn't easy for me. You need to know that."

Adelaide rubs her eyelids as if guilt can be detected in her gaze, and just as easily buffed away.

Henry flaps his wings and stretches his neck to the sky, offering a mangled cry to the morning. Adelaide tries to imagine breaking that neck, but she can't find the strength to reach for him. He returns to the woodpile, searching for more concealed insects.

Adelaide looks down at Moffit.

The hen gazes across the yard, though if she is looking at anything in particular, Adelaide cannot discern. She places her hands on Moffit's body to warm the trembling bird.

Adelaide wonders if the children are awake. And if so, are they as surprised as she was to find that they had fallen asleep in her bed? Will she enter the cabin only to discover them hidden in their tent, once again hesitant and uneasy?

Adelaide strokes Moffit's head.

She stares past the garden and into the forest where the fallen snow has settled into the creases of branches like soft white nests.

Her hand moves to Moffit's neck, massaging beneath her beak with her thumb.

Adelaide closes her eyes and listens to the forest. There is little to hear beyond the sound of Henry and Zelda scratching at the snow, but when she pushes her hearing into the morning, she detects bare branches on the other side of the cabin, creaking in the morning breeze.

She moves her other hand to the top of Moffit's shoulders.

And as she pushes her hearing even *farther*, Adelaide believes she can hear sheets of ice creaking and shifting on the surface of the river.

She imagines plunging her body into the cold, and she snaps Moffit's neck.

She's done as she must.

But she can do no more today.

The children eat with greedy mouths, their faces flushed and grateful. Adelaide divides her portion among the two emptying plates.

She cannot join them for breakfast this time.

The stench of blood and grease permeates her cabin, and so Adelaide leaves the children to their meal and steps outside.

Adelaide gasps for fresh air, forcing the icy chill into her lungs with rushed breaths that do not satisfy. She doesn't doubt her decision, but oh, how her heart aches. Her fingers are still slick with chicken fat, and Moffit's blood stains the creases of her knuckles. She buffs it away as best she can.

There is no such thing as a magnificent death. Everyone, and everything, dies. Adelaide understands this more than most, but it hurts all the same.

She cannot look at Henry and Zelda today—perhaps never again—and Adelaide passes them without so much as a glance or a word as she walks toward the river. She turns at the bank, following the frozen river downstream, to her secret spot. She longs to hear its symphonic eddy once more and hopes that in that deepest part of the river, the water still flows.

The last time she was here, the weather was warmer, and she did not dread a dip in its depths. The leaves were crimson then, the sun bright. There will be no red leaves today, no crown to weave into her bun, and no pills in her pocket. Just an old, gutless woman sitting by a frozen river.

As she approaches, Adelaide is relieved to discover the water still churning and spinning. She sits beneath the barren maple tree, watching the slow rotation of bubbles and ice chips, and tries to calm her quaking fingers. One more day. That's all she can rely on. She can no longer plan for next week, next month. Only one more day. And even that small task is a burden. Today, at least, she has fed the children. And when River and Little Bird awake tomorrow with rumbling bellies, Adelaide still has two more chickens.

She buries her face in her hands, massages her temples. She presses too hard and will likely bruise, but she does not release. A small consequence for murdering Moffit. She deserves more than a bruise. Some farmer she's become, in mourning over a goddamn chicken.

Across the river, Adelaide spots motion and looks up to find a small brown hare staring back at her. Its fur is chestnut brown, its belly cream. The rabbit stands on its hind legs, front paws in a V, ears the color of strawberry jam. For a long moment, they regard each other. Eventually, the rabbit deems Adelaide no threat, turns, and hops leisurely into the trees.

There was a time when Adelaide would have hunted it down, dined on bunny stew. But today, all Adelaide can think is: Run, little rabbit. Run fast and far from the likes of me.

Though still early in the day, the sky has darkened, and Adelaide steps carefully over roots and stones on her way back to her cabin. A storm is coming. The air is icy, and the updraft of wind whisks the stark gray branches toward a dampening sky. She'd been too distracted to notice earlier, and Adelaide quickens her pace. She hopes the children won't be frightened, but then reminds herself that this is likely their first storm for which they will have shelter. A real home. Because of her.

Adelaide smiles when she thinks of the children. *Her* children. She should not have left them alone for so long. It is not their fault that Moffit is dead. It is not their fault that Adelaide let her cupboards go bare this winter. It is her burden, and hers alone.

As she approaches the cabin, Adelaide spots a car parked in her driveway. The vehicle is empty. No driver, no passengers.

It's the men. Must be.

And the children are home alone.

Adelaide wrings her hands, trying to decide if she should sneak quietly to a window and assess the situation, or if she should charge down her front door, unleashing a holy hell of wild madness upon the men. If the children have taught her one thing, it is that men are easily spooked by a little bit of crazy. Yes, she thinks as she grabs a fallen tree branch, holding it like a sickle, she, too, can be a beast.

Adelaide leaps forward, charging through the brush. Her cabin grows larger before her, looming, dominating the sky. The tree branch rocks and sways against her shoulder, bruising, cutting, but Adelaide feels nothing. She is an animal now. A fierce protector. A mother bear. Adelaide hollers a battle cry into the sky. She screeches and hoots and turns every noise she's ever heard in the mountains into a single roar of fury.

Heavy flurries begin to fall, peppering Adelaide with frigid pellets as she flings open her front door, releasing a mighty howl from the depths of her lungs. No words. Just vowels and syllables.

Adelaide crouches low, weapon brandished, teeth bared, knees bloodied.

Feral.

She hears a small child's cry, though not that of River or Little Bird. Adelaide blinks the snow from her eyes and sees a woman recoiling into the corner of her sofa, comforting a terrified little girl with a yellow ribbon in her blonde ponytail.

Adelaide stands, her mouth slack, her mind empty. The woman stares at her with eyes as threatening as the approaching storm—dark, bewitching, and oh so familiar.

The woman screams at Adelaide, "Dear God, Mother! What's gotten into you?"

14

The flames lick the air with orange tongues. Adelaide sips her hot tea and watches the fireplace because it is easier than looking into her daughter's eyes.

"I need you to answer me."

Adelaide is silent as a burning log collapses, pitching smoldering ash into the air. It burns out before landing on the hearth.

"Goddamn it, Mother. Who is the baby food for?"

"I owe you no explanations, Catherine."

"The hell you don't."

Wind howls outside the windows, throwing fistfuls of snow against the glass, and Adelaide chances a look into her bedroom. Just behind the clean, yellow-ribboned little girl playing games on a screen, two faces peer out from beneath Adelaide's bed. She gives a small nod and promptly turns to face her daughter, hoping the children understand enough to stay quiet.

Adelaide smiles. "It's so nice to finally see your face," Adelaide says.

Catherine pinches her eyebrows. "Don't start."

"I'm only saying I miss you."

"You're saying more than that."

The two women watch the fire in silence.

"What's her name?" Adelaide motions to the little girl.

"You know her name."

Catherine is right. She *does* know the girl's name. But she's never before met her granddaughter, and the name, heard only once and very long ago, escapes her. The girl's skin is so fair that the light from the fireplace seems to shine right through it. She watches something on the handheld screen in rapt fascination.

"Who is the baby food for, Mother?"

Adelaide pauses a moment before responding and folds her hands in her lap. "It's for me."

Catherine swings her head toward Adelaide, eyes rolling so severely it's a wonder she doesn't fall down.

"For you," she confirms.

"Yes, for me. It's easier on my gums."

"And I suppose the baby formula is for you as well. And the cloth diapers."

Adelaide shrugs her shoulders. It's not so out of the ordinary, she imagines. Growing old is much like becoming a child again. But she seeks to change the subject nonetheless.

"Your daughter," Adelaide begins.

"Alice. *Your granddaughter.*"

"That's right. Alice. How old—"

"Five."

"Five. That's a great age."

"Was it, Mother?

Adelaide sighs. "Thank you for bringing supplies."

"And I brought the wine you asked for." At last, Catherine smiles.

Adelaide smiles back. "Wonderful. We can share a glass tonight. That would be lovely."

"Actually," Catherine says, nesting her mug between her thighs, "we're not staying long."

"Not even for supper?"

"No. I . . ." Catherine's words trail away, and she seems to have lost them. She takes another sip of her tea to fill the silence. "We're moving, actually. Derek was transferred to another branch."

For the first time, Catherine seems hesitant to look her mother in the eyes, and instead ruffles Alice's hair. But Adelaide is patient, and she waits for eye contact before responding.

"Where are you going?"

"Chicago."

Adelaide pinches the bridge of her nose. "That sounds ghastly."

"We'll learn to love it." She grasps Alice's knee and gives it a little shake. "Won't we?" Alice finds her screen more riveting than her mother and doesn't respond.

"That's very far away. Will you be coming back?"

Catherine leans back into the sofa and studies the rotted wood of the ceiling. Adelaide hopes she doesn't judge her too harshly.

"No."

Adelaide twists her knuckles, and though it hurts, it's more pleasant than this conversation.

"What about my supplies?"

Another log in the fireplace pops and collapses, sending small plumes of soot into the cabin.

"I brought you double supplies this time."

Adelaide doesn't doubt this. She glances at the stockpile of groceries in her kitchen. For the children, she is grateful. But it feels like accepting blood money.

"You didn't send a supply list last season," Catherine states.

"No."

"You didn't need anything."

"No."

Catherine sighs heavily through her teeth, the sound like two passing planes in the distance, and says no more about it.

"Well, whatever you could possibly need until spring is in the kitchen," Catherine says, reaching into her pocket and withdrawing a piece of yellow paper. "And take this as well. A friend in town said she'd help with supply runs down the road. I left her some cash for her trouble." Catherine stands, but Adelaide cannot look at her. "It's the best I can do."

Adelaide stares at the scrap of paper. A name and address scribbled in pencil. A stranger. An outsider.

Catherine plucks the screen from Alice's lap. The girl frowns but concedes. She then stands and takes her mother's hand, shooting Adelaide an accusatory glance from behind the safety of her mother's thigh.

Catherine waits in silence. For a grand farewell, Adelaide imagines. But she cannot stand. Her muscles have turned to jelly, her bones to noodles. Adelaide places her hands over her kneecaps to stop them from trembling.

Catherine throws up her hands. "Okay, Mother. Enjoy the pureed carrots."

Adelaide watches two shadows retreat as her daughter and granddaughter move toward the door. The hinge creaks as it flies open, taken by the wind, and a gust of frozen air assaults the cabin. Her pots shake. Her curtains dance.

"Wait!" Adelaide cries, tears breaking in a torrent down her cheeks. "Not yet. Not like this."

Catherine taps her fingernails against her wineglass. Adelaide taps her fingertips, too, but her nails are whittled away, and instead of a clean, crisp sound, she leaves only smudges of dirt against her glass.

In the living room, Alice dozes on the sofa, head nestled between two pillows that have seen better days.

"I'm glad you stayed," Adelaide says softly, watching the girl's blonde head rise and fall with her breaths.

"Mhm."

"It won't delay your trip?"

Catherine spins the wineglass between her palms. "We'll make it work." She turns to the window. Streaks of rain are the only reprieve in the blackness outside. "It *is* nasty out there," Catherine says. "Can't argue with that."

"I'm sure you could manage."

Catherine glares at her mother for a small moment before laughing. Sometimes wine is the best therapy, and Adelaide is ever so grateful that she brought it.

"So, I have to ask," Catherine says, "what's with the fort in the living room?"

Adelaide had completely forgotten about the children's sleep tent, now merely a pile of blankets and pillows.

"Oh, that?"

Catherine laughs. "Yes, that! Are you planning a camping trip with bedsheets and baby food?"

Adelaide nods to herself, wondering if she should confess. But Catherine would never understand.

"Something like that, I suppose."

"Mother."

"Daughter."

Catherine leans back in the chair, her smile dissipating with the flicker of the fire. She pours a little more wine into each of their glasses. "I'm worried about you."

"You insult me." Adelaide takes a large gulp and half her glass disappears.

"You're acting very strange," Catherine says. "I've never seen you like this."

Adelaide holds up a hand to stop her, but she continues.

"First you charge into the house like a madwoman with a stick. You're requesting baby food and diapers. You're making forts in your living room. If it were anyone but me, you'd be locked up right about now."

"But it *is* you."

"I'm allowed to be concerned."

"The hell you are."

"Goddamn it, Mother."

"Goddamn yourself."

Catherine nods. "Good talk." She places her glass in the middle of the table. "I need to use your bathroom."

"You know where it is."

Catherine groans. "I hate that outhouse."

"My fancy daughter needs a fancy place to piss?"

Catherine takes a deep breath and places her hands on her hips as she stands. She looks to Alice asleep on the sofa. "I suppose I should wake her. And now I have the pleasure of teaching my daughter to squat over a hole in the ground."

"Take my coat," Adelaide offers. "And when you come back, we'll finish our talk."

Catherine takes the coat hanging by the door and shrugs into it. "This is no place for children," she mutters, rousing her daughter, and bundling her in the nearest blanket. Adelaide holds open the door, bracing against the wind before easing it quietly into place behind them.

Adelaide waits by the door for a moment, and then rushes to the paper sacks on the floor, searching for food for River and Little Bird. She finds a bag of chips, grabs them, but thinks better of it. Chips would be too loud, she thinks, and returns them to the grocery sack. She finds a soft loaf of bread and quickly rips the tie from the plastic. Adelaide burrows her fingers into the crust, pulling out four slices in one handful, and dashes to her bedroom calling their names in a rushed whisper.

"River. Little Bird. I have something for you."

Adelaide thrusts her hands under the bed, and the children waste no time in plucking the bread from her fingers. Little Bird peers out at her, grinning, grasping his bread in one tight fist, the small gray elephant in the other. He begins to wiggle out, but Adelaide throws up her hands and shakes her head. Little Bird scowls. From beneath the bed, River's voice chirps softly. A few syllables of their special-speak and Little Bird retreats into shadow.

Adelaide rushes back to the kitchen table, stations herself in her chair, and grabs her wineglass, swallowing a few deep gulps to still her heart. She can't stop smiling. But she *must* stop smiling before Catherine sees her and calls the Crazy Police to pick her up this very night. She can't believe she thought the children young enough to need formula and baby food. She scolds herself for being so blind. They are small, but these children are no toddlers.

Catherine's feet clatter on the front steps, and she whips open the door, Alice draped across her shoulder. The wind gusts around them like a cyclone, and Catherine struggles to close the door. She looks at Adelaide. "Worth it."

The two women laugh, and Adelaide is glad for the excuse to smile.

Catherine lays Alice on the sofa, tucking the blanket around her, before returning to the kitchen table. She shivers and plucks her glass from the table.

"It's cold out there," Catherine says.

"Plenty warm in here."

Adelaide and Catherine talk well into the night about Derek, his new promotion, the great migration to Chicago, and of course, Alice. Adelaide is grateful to have known her granddaughter, if only for a night. But the liability of River and Little Bird weighs heavily on her mind, and she chooses quiet moments in the conversation to peer over her shoulder and make sure they are still hidden.

"What are you looking for, Mom?"

Adelaide turns back to her daughter. "Just checking that the bedroom window is shut tight."

In the living room, a sleeping Alice coughs. She sniffles and wipes her nose with her palm before falling asleep once more.

"She sounds sick. I hope it's nothing serious."

"Just your garden-variety cold, Mom. She's fine."

Sometimes the conversation with Catherine flows like a warm river in the summertime. And sometimes it stalls, heavy, lumbering like a winter storm. Adelaide doesn't mind. It's been a long time since she's sat and talked with her daughter.

"You could come with us, you know," Catherine says.

"With you? Where?"

Catherine sighs. "Chicago, Mother."

"Heavens, no."

"We have the room."

"Absolutely not."

"We can help you get some things packed. I can't leave you here like this."

"I won't hear another word of it."

Catherine leans back and pushes her palms into her eyes. If there was any wine left, Adelaide would have refilled their glasses by now. With the pleasantry of alcohol long gone, real life creeps back into the conversation.

Adelaide clears her throat and corrects her tone. "My life is here. Everything I know is here."

"Everything you *chose* is here. There's a big difference. You chose this. Even if it meant losing me, you chose *this*."

"You were a blessing."

"I was an affliction."

Adelaide leans forward, her eyes sharp, focused. "Don't you ever say that." Her voice is low, angry. Not angry at Catherine, but angry nonetheless.

"Don't worry, Mother. I have no more tears. But let's not lie to each other. Not anymore. That's exactly what I was. I was the silver lining—at best—to the worst experience of your life."

Adelaide feels the old man in her forest as they speak. Somewhere in these woods, he sleeps.

"I never should have told you. That was my burden, not yours."

"Knowledge is power. Isn't that what you said?"

"But ignorance is bliss."

The clock ticks from Adelaide's bedroom, filling the space between them. *Tsk-tsk-tsk.*

"Well," Catherine says, "I feel neither powerful nor blissful, so where does that leave me?"

Adelaide is tired. Her eyelids droop, and her mind is heavy and slow. She no longer has the right words. Maybe she never did. Communication between the two of them has always been distorted. Words are misinterpreted, rearranged, and never in the right sequence. They may as well be speaking in chirps and grunts.

Catherine sighs. "I'm going to sleep now. We'll talk in the morning."

Adelaide nearly offers her bed before remembering that River and Little Bird are hidden beneath. To her relief, Catherine moves Alice to the blankets on the floor, and takes the sofa before Adelaide can come up with a solution.

Adelaide blows out the lantern on her way to the bedroom and pulls a wool blanket from the shelf of her closet, tucking it discreetly under the bed. She slips beneath her sheets, careful not to put all her weight in one spot, and dangles her arm over the side of the mattress. A small hand squeezes her fingers. Adelaide squeezes back.

Outside, the wind has grown still. It seems the storm has finally passed.

Somewhere deep in the woods, a howl.

Adelaide's eyes snap open. The wild woman is back. The little hand holding her fingers unlatches, disappearing beneath the mattress, and Adelaide is left alone with the sound. Tonight, it is sorrowful, lonely. Adelaide hopes the wild woman found shelter from the storm. Somewhere, somehow. Her calls have become a sort of anchor for Adelaide. A segmented part of her own mind, lost and forever wandering the forest. She listens to the cry as it echoes across the landscape, and hopes Catherine is asleep. And if she isn't, perhaps she'll think it merely a coyote.

🌺

The girl listens to all the sleep-breathing. There is the woman above them sleep-breathing, the new woman on the sofa sleep-breathing, and much smaller sleep-breathing coming from the little girl on the floor.

Brother crawls out. The girl doesn't want him to get hurt, but she wants to see, too, so she follows.

Long, dark hair falls over the side of the sofa, and the girl stops to stare at it. Brother stops, too. The new woman's hair is soft and straight, like the grass that hangs down from the big trees by the water. The new woman is scary, but she is asleep, and so they are safe.

The girl is not fast enough to stop brother from touching the new woman's hair. She whispers a stop sound to him and he pulls his hand back. He smells his fingertips and smiles. The girl smells brother's fingertips—they smell like the small pointy flowers that grow in a big bunch. The girl doesn't understand how hair can smell like flowers, but she wants her hair to smell like flowers, too. Mother knows everything. When they are with mother again, she will ask mother to make her hair smell like flowers.

The new woman's face is a little bit scary, even when she sleeps. Her eyes look mad and her mouth looks mad. The girl wonders how long she will be here and hopes not very long.

The girl looks away from the new woman who is mad when she sleeps, and crouches beside the little girl on the floor. Brother sits by her so he can look, too. Her hair is the color of the tall grass that's fun to chew on. The girl rubs her fingers on the little girl's arm. Her skin is very light, like river sand, and even softer. Brother gasps. She shushes him, and he shushes. The girl smells her fingers. The little girl on the floor does not smell like the small pointy flowers that grow in a big bunch. She smells like berries.

Brother leans closer to the floor, and the girl whispers the not-so-close sound, but brother doesn't listen. He gets even closer. The girl does not get as close to the little girl on the floor as brother does. Sometimes she is not as brave as brother. The little girl on the floor has long hairs on her eyes that flutter as she sleeps. Brother leans in to touch them but changes his mind. He touches her cheek, her ear, her nose.

And then the little girl on the floor opens her mouth and sneezes on brother's face.

Brother is still, and his sister is still, and the little girl on the floor did not wake up and is still.

Brother looks at the girl, his face wet and sparkling in the firelight. Eyes big. Teeth showing. And then they are laughing and rushing back to hide beneath the bed before they wake up the new woman on the sofa and the little girl on the floor and make them mad.

❧

Morning came too fast for Adelaide.

She boils water in a cast-iron pot over the fireplace as Catherine helps Alice from the floor.

"You won't stay for tea?"

Catherine drops a folded blanket onto the sofa, fluffing the corners into a perfect square. "We've got to get back."

"Would Alice like some breakfast?"

"We'll get something on the way. We don't want to use up your food. You'll be needing it."

Adelaide nods, glancing to the small child-shaped shadows beneath her bed.

"I suppose so." Adelaide runs her hands up her hair, straightening her bun. "Coyotes were really carrying on last night."

"We didn't hear anything."

"Oh," Adelaide says, surprised but relieved. "That's good."

Catherine stands and looks at Adelaide. Neither woman seems to have the right words.

"I have something for you," Adelaide says, walking toward her cabinet.

"I don't need anything."

"Yes, you do."

"I really don't. We're all packed, and I don't have room for anything else."

"You have room for this."

Catherine sighs loudly, but Adelaide ignores her, pulling down a stack of torn papers, tied with a length of pink yarn. The remnants of her diary.

"Take this with you."

Catherine accepts the bundle, examining what little writing can be seen. "What is it?"

"It's something I've held on to for a very long time. I almost lost it recently. This is all I could salvage." Adelaide sighs. "But it was never mine. It was always yours."

"Mom—"

"Just take it with you," Adelaide says, folding Catherine's fingers around the paper. "Once you've settled, make some time to look through it."

"Are you crying, Mom?"

"No."

"Yes, you are."

Adelaide waves her hand in the air. "Pay no mind." She turns to Alice. "Young lady, come give your grandmother a hug."

The little girl tucks into Adelaide's embrace, hesitant to uncross her arms, but Adelaide is not offended.

Catherine raises the paper bundle in the air. "I'll look through it," she says. "Once we're settled."

"I hope you will."

Catherine smiles and steps forward to hug her mother, little Alice trapped and struggling between them. Adelaide holds on to Catherine for as long as she will allow.

"I love you, Mom."

"You too."

"Take care of yourself out here."

"Always do."

Adelaide stands in the doorway until she can no longer see the snowdrifts left by the wheels of their car. From within the fireplace, the kettle whistles. Behind her, Little Bird sneezes.

15

The day that Little Bird fell ill, Adelaide did not notice. She spent the afternoon unpacking all the glorious supplies that Catherine had bestowed. Her little cabin in the woods was a veritable grocery store, filled with delicate fresh fruits, canned vegetables, beans and all manner of bottled goods. Rice and powdered milk and preserved meats and fragrant teas. Adelaide unpacked instead of mourning the absence of her daughter. She snacked instead of worrying about next season's supply run. She cleaned with her new disinfectants, and wiped with her new dishcloths, and replaced the clock batteries, and she didn't notice anything odd about Little Bird.

The next day brought a lethargy to Little Bird, and a loss of appetite that Adelaide might have noticed had River not snatched the bread and cheese slices from his plate when Adelaide's back was turned. She did not notice that he could no longer hold on to his gray elephant, the animal slipping from his fingers. Adelaide tended to Henry and Zelda and shoveled snow from the doorway, and even scooped some snow into cups, topped with a drizzle of honey, for the children. Adelaide did not notice that Little Bird's cup melted into sticky water that leaked through the cracks between the floorboards when he knocked the cup from the table.

But this morning, River shoves Adelaide's shoulder until she wakes. The girl's eyes are large, her face wet with tears. She leads Adelaide to the living room where a barely conscious Little Bird lies strewn across the floor, his face slick with sweat, his skin hotter than the fireplace.

Today, three days since Catherine's departure, Adelaide notices Little Bird.

His legs dangle askew from the folds of Adelaide's elbows, his sweat dampening her coat, as she rushes through the front door. River trails behind, stumbling over snow ridges. The sun is warm today, a glorious complement to the frigidity of the air. But lovely as it is, Little Bird does not need warmth. Little Bird needs cold.

Adelaide runs to the river, but finds it still frozen, so she turns at the bank, heading to her secret spot. She hopes the grand canopy will bestow a miracle on her Little Bird.

Behind her, River squawks and yelps.

"Follow me, little one. Stay right close. We're almost there. A little farther. Can you make it?"

River chirps. It's a *Yes*.

"Good girl, River. We must help your brother now. I need you to be a strong sister."

Little Bird is listless in Adelaide's arms. His skin is aflame, his eyes open but seeing nothing. She runs faster.

Adelaide doesn't remember the trail to the eddy being so strenuous. It's as if the heat from his little body has penetrated her skin, her bones, and she is plummeting to the ground. At this rate, they may only reach the eddy by way of crawling on all fours.

They arrive at last, and Adelaide collapses to her knees, laying Little Bird down onto the chilled earth.

How blind she has been, so lost in her tedious chores that she has failed to notice *this* for days. Some mother she is. Some second chance.

She places her hand on his forehead, and though his body floods the clearing with heat, his skin is cold and wet.

"Little Bird," she whispers, "look at me."

He does not.

Adelaide pushes open his eyelids and it seems Little Bird is not looking at anything at all.

"Little Bird, River is here. Your sister. Your sister is here, and she's right beside you. Can you look at her?"

He trembles.

Adelaide places her hand on River's shoulders.

"Your brother is going to be okay. But he's sick, and we must help him feel better." Adelaide hopes she understands. "You can trust me. Have I ever let you down?"

As the words escape her lips, shame drops like a steel trap to the deepest part of Adelaide's gut.

"River," she says, enunciating every word clearly, including the girl's name. "River, I need you to gather snow and wrap it around Little Bird's body. Can you do that?"

Adelaide gathers small handfuls of snow, tucking them against his thighs, under his neck, in his open hand. She looks at River. "Just like this. We need to cool him down. He is too hot."

As River takes up the task of mounding snow around her brother, Adelaide holds her fingers to his wrist to count his heart rate. The number seems impossible. Astronomical. This cannot be right.

She places her hand on his warm chest, and his heart thunders beneath her palm. Adelaide can't remember the last time she was sick. It doesn't happen out here in the mountains, secluded as she is.

She thinks of Alice, her granddaughter, coughing on her sofa, her floor, only days ago.

"Garden-variety cold," her daughter had said. No doubt. But these children have never before been exposed to other people, and their other-people germs. They are defenseless against an infection in their sinuses, a virus in their lungs. Adelaide scoops Little Bird into her arms, tucking fresh snow beneath his ears and against his neck. He moans. She buffs it into his chest like a menthol rub, and smears it along the soles of his feet, squeezing them with her quaking hands.

Everything is so large around them—tree trunks wide as cars; the canopy above, bony and expansive; the frozen river stretching from one bank to the next; the narrow dirt road and the mountains that look down from great heights; the snow falling from somewhere so profound and otherworldly, it is a wonder it falls to earth at all.

And the three of them—so small and insignificant in the middle of all this grandeur. Forgotten. Abandoned together. One sick, so very sick. And Adelaide unable to help. She lifts her head to the bare branches above, locking her stiff fingers together so tightly they may never unlatch. And she begs for someone—anyone—to help her Little Bird.

✿

The girl is scared, and she is no mother. If she were a mother, she wouldn't be scared. If she were a mother, she would know how to help.

Something is wrong with brother. She feels his hurt like there is something wrong with her, too. The girl wonders if she is strong enough to take away brother's hurt, and she tries to hold on to it, tries to make it bigger, heavier. She feels hot, then cold, and she rolls her eyes back into her head, and tries as hard as she can to feel all the bad things for brother. But when she looks at brother, he is not better. She did not take away enough of his hurt.

She can feel brother slipping further, like he is going away forever.

The girl moves her lips and her tongue and tries to distract herself with all the woman sounds she has learned. The words she and brother used to practice, before he got very sick. She makes the *ooo* sound and the *eee* sound and the *mmm* sound, and many other sounds, but she can't put them together in her mouth at the same time, like the woman does. The girl wonders what *she* must sound like to the woman. The woman makes funny sounds that aren't words. But maybe the woman thinks she and brother make funny sounds that aren't words, too.

The girl leans against brother's damp body and rests her head on his lap. She has so many things to figure out, but she can't think about anything anymore. She is too scared. So she falls asleep on brother, twining her fingers into his fingers.

❀

Adelaide spends the afternoon dripping water into Little Bird's mouth. When he begins to shiver, she holds him until he stops. When his body becomes a furnace once again, she places him back onto the snow.

Little Bird opens his eyes, he whispers something to his sister, and River immediately stands and runs away. Adelaide does not know where the girl is going, and she does not call after her. If River knows what's best for her, she will run far away from this place. Far away from Adelaide and the tragedy she has brought upon these children. But soon enough, River reappears under the canopy by the eddy, returning to Little Bird, food in hand. For the first time all day, Little Bird sits up and eats the bread his sister has brought him.

River kneels beside Adelaide, knees touching, and Adelaide resists the urge to scoop the girl into her arms, squeeze her tightly, and thank her for not abandoning them. Abandoning *her*. Adelaide is beginning to feel as though she needs the children more than the children need her.

Little Bird finishes his meal and vomits into the snowbank.

16

When the sun begins to set, the wind becomes too cold for Adelaide and she scoops up a sleeping Little Bird, carrying him back toward her cabin. River follows. For every step Adelaide takes, there is a smaller, child-size step just behind her.

And a larger, adult-size step on the other side of the frozen river.

Adelaide scans the bank but sees nothing—only a spattering of snow adrift on the breeze.

The amber glow of her windows is like a beacon, promising warmth, shelter. Little Bird shifts in her arms but remains asleep.

Again, a noise from across the river.

Adelaide stops so suddenly that River runs into the back of her legs.

River begins to growl a low, rumbling hum. Such a fierce sound to escape the lips of a child. River drops to all fours, her body rigid. She curls her back, staring across the river at something Adelaide cannot see in the darkness.

Safeguarding her homestead has always been Adelaide's primary concern. But right now, the sweltering child lying unconscious in her arms is her *only* priority, and so Adelaide turns away from the river and continues up the path that leads them home.

River follows closely behind, lobbing threats and spittle into the unknown.

River slumps beside Adelaide on the sofa, tucking beneath her arm, and Adelaide pulls the girl closer. Little Bird lays motionless across Adelaide's thighs, the *bump-bump-bump* of his racing heart hammering her skin. All she can do is stroke his moist hair, blow cool breaths across his face, and feel the *bump-bump-bumps*.

Adelaide fetches a wet rag from the side table and wrings the excess water into a bowl before laying it across his forehead. She can keep him cool when he sweats, and she can embrace him when he shivers. But there is nothing more she can do for Little Bird; there is no medicine to be found here. Little Bird no longer eats, no longer drinks. What she forces into his mouth simply drips from the corner of his lips. She fears he may soon begin to inhale the water, and so she has stopped trying.

A few miles down the mountain, there is a town. And a hospital. She was there once, after her accident in the garden. She listened to their beeping monitors, swallowed their bland pudding, and accepted their narcotics.

She could go there now; they might make it. If River could keep up, that is. And if Adelaide could carry Little Bird for miles over mountains and snow. It's certainly possible. But what then? Adelaide would arrive at the emergency room with two dirty, naked children—one nearly dead, the other quaking with fear and barking at the nurses.

She would lose them for sure. And that can't happen.

A shadow approaches her living room window. Palms against the glass. Face obscured by night.

Adelaide holds her breath and tightens her grasp around the children as she studies the silhouette.

This time, it is not one of the men from the farm. The figure is smaller, thinner, shoulders bent and slumped forward against the glass.

It's all come down to this. She can avoid it no more.

The wild woman is here, on the porch, staring through the window at Adelaide and the children on her sofa. The feral mother. Both thief and beast.

But there is no snarl on the wild woman's face this night. Her eyes are hollow cutouts above her sunken cheeks, and her fingertips leave spots of fog against the glass. She does not spit. She does not scream. She places her forehead against the window and Adelaide fights the urge to let her inside. The children tucked within her arms are not her blood. She has failed them, harmed them, though all she'd wanted was to protect them. She is a curse, and she should have died in that river so many weeks ago.

If she had any guts inside her at all, she would rip the door from the hinges and place these children in the arms of their *real* mother. But she is a coward, and instead, she hugs them closer.

The wild woman makes no effort to break into the cabin. She does not bang against the walls or attempt to smash the window. The wild woman drops her hand and turns, her matted hair leaving streaks across the glass. Adelaide imagines she will sit on the porch all night, and Adelaide thinks that would be okay. If the men show their faces around here tonight, they will have *two* angry mothers to deal with.

Somewhere outside an owl trills, its hollow song swaying from tree to tree. Beyond that, silence. Miles of powdery snow has smothered all sound, insulating her cabin from the rest of the forest, but tonight, Adelaide is not sheltered. This particular night, she is forsaken.

Adelaide no longer feels Little Bird's heartbeat against her thigh, his *bump-bump-bumps* evaporating into the soundless winter's night, and for a moment, her heart stops as well, but she can't bring herself to look down.

Perhaps she's wrong. Dear god, let her be wrong.

When Adelaide finds the strength to place her hand against his forehead, she knows for sure, and she bites her tongue to keep from crying out. To keep from waking River. To keep from alerting the wild woman outside her window. But Adelaide doesn't know how long she can stifle her screams.

She wants to squeeze him, beat his chest, beat her own, howl into the night, gnash her teeth, cry until the sky splits open and the trees blow away and there is nothing left in this very spot but earth and rock. And no children ever existed in this spot, and no heart was ever torn from its chest in this spot.

Adelaide hates. It wells in her skin, this hate. It grows taller and rips through her scalp. This hate is consuming, and submitting to its power is the only thing she wants to do right now.

But next to the dead child in her lap is a very live child who needs her now more than ever.

Adelaide takes a breath, forcing the oxygen into the deepest part of her lungs. She flexes her fingers, tries to calm herself. The hate in her heart does not leave, but it goes still for just a moment.

Adelaide looks to the window, and the wild woman is once again plastered to the glass. She knows. Of course she does. The wild woman locks eyes with Adelaide, and Adelaide freezes. She is a murderer at worst. Negligent at best. And the wild woman sees her for what she is.

Adelaide looks down at Little Bird for the first time. She turns him over in her lap, and his body acquiesces. Adelaide touches his small fists, strokes his eyebrows, runs her thumb across his soft lashes. She does not cry.

Perhaps Adelaide is dead herself. She wonders where her brain has gone. Where her heart has gone. She is steel and cement, not even human. She pushes a few stray hairs from his face and leans forward to place her forehead against his own.

Outside, the wild woman begins to howl.

Adelaide loosens her grip on Little Bird. There is nothing to hold on to any longer.

River stirs, and Adelaide places her hand on the girl's back, feeling her heartbeat through her ribs. It is strong and insistent. If River hasn't yet become ill, perhaps she'll be okay.

River turns over and peers at Adelaide, rubbing the sleep from her eyes. She sits up, looking to the window and to her mother beyond. Then River sees Little Bird and shrieks into the night.

Adelaide heaves the little girl into her arms, and buries her face in the child's unruly hair, while outside, the wild woman bellows for them both.

River turns over and peers at Adelaide, rubbing the sleep from her

17

The girl watches the woman dig. Not with her hands but with something shiny. It looks heavy and dangerous, and when the woman stumbles and falls, the girl jumps.

Something happened to brother last night. Something bad. When she woke up, she felt the woman's big hurt, and she felt mother's big hurt, but she couldn't feel brother's hurt at all.

Brother is asleep in the blanket now.

Blanket.

The girl knows the word, but her mouth cannot say it. She will practice more with brother when he wakes up.

The girl wanted to see brother this morning, but when she lifted the blanket, she made the woman mad. The girl doesn't like it when the woman is mad, so she didn't lift the blanket again.

She talks to brother, but brother doesn't talk back. The girl hopes he hasn't gone away forever.

The woman looks mad. Or maybe she looks sad. The girl can't always tell the difference. She thinks maybe there isn't such a big difference.

The woman lifts brother, and his foot slips out from the blanket. It is the color of the pale rain. Brother is cold. That must be why he is in the blanket.

The woman puts brother in the hole, and the girl stands. She asks the woman why she is doing that, but the woman doesn't answer. The woman makes a sound at her, but the girl doesn't know what the sound means. She knows brother sounds, not woman sounds.

Brother is in the hole now, in the square forest inside the forest. The girl screams at the woman, and the woman screams back.

The woman is hurting brother, making him go away forever, and the girl is not a mother and so the girl does not know what to do, how to stop her. Now the woman is putting dirt on top of brother in the hole and he won't be able to breathe and the girl is screaming and the woman is crying and the girl wants mother to come quick and make everything okay.

The skies are darker now, and the clouds are growling, and the girl smells the rain before it falls and it is falling now and brother is getting wet. He is under the ground in the square forest and he can't breathe and he is getting wet and the girl is yelling at the woman—bad things, mad things, sad things—but the woman isn't listening.

The woman runs toward her, and the girl fights back, but the woman is so strong.

A voice inside the girl's mind tells her to stop screaming, but she can't.

The woman carries the girl toward the cabin and the girl doesn't understand. Brother has not gone away forever—he is *right there*, outside, under the ground, and it is raining, and he is wet, and she doesn't understand. But the woman is not mad, only sad, and she holds her like a mother, and the girl lays her head on the woman's shoulder and whispers to brother to please get up. But he doesn't.

The woman rushes inside and shuts the door, and the girl slides from her arms.

The girl pounds on the window and pounds on the walls, but the woman isn't listening—she has curled herself into a ball on the floor, and it's almost like she has gone away forever.

But the girl can still feel her. She aches with all of the woman's hurt. It is never-ending, stretching on and on like moving water. The woman's hurt is hot on the girl's skin like the burning sun, and it fills the air like pale rain.

The girl begins to tremble, her fingers like small branches in a big wind. She's never felt this way before, and the girl wants to scream. She wants to tear off her skin and pull out her hair so this feeling goes away. She wants to chew on her fingers and poke at her eyes and go back to sleep so she doesn't feel the woman's hurt anymore. Or her own.

The girl curls her fist and pushes it against her lips, suckling her knuckles. She looks up but there is no sky. Only a wood sky with no sun and no clouds.

Something is different today. Different from yesterday. She thinks tomorrow will be different, too.

🌺

Adelaide cannot feel her toes.

As she sits here now, on her sofa which has become stained over the years by so much dirt, tea, and sweat that it's practically a new color altogether, Adelaide realizes she can't feel her hands either. Her heart, it seems, is numb as well—finally, a blessing.

Something hums in her cabin, but it may be in her head. Her aging mind. Her witch soul. She pushes into the cushion and listens to River. The girl is napping in the bedroom, and though it is late in the day, Adelaide thinks that today, that is alright. Today, the girl watched Adelaide bury her brother. Sleep, child.

Adelaide wonders how much the girl understands. Does she realize her brother is dead, and never coming back? And if so, does she believe Adelaide caused him harm? Perhaps she did. Adelaide buffs her forehead to force the guilt away. *She did not cause this.* It was an acci-dent. She couldn't have known, couldn't have prevented it.

But the simple truth remains: if Adelaide had left them in the woods with their feral mother, Little Bird would still be alive.

She glances to the child slumbering in her bed. River's arm drapes over the side, and from her fingers dangles the butter-yellow knitted cap. Clasped tightly to her chest is the small gray elephant. Little Bird's elephant. If Adelaide had thought of it earlier, she would have buried it with him. But maybe this is better.

Adelaide walks past the fireplace that once fascinated Little Bird. She walks past the rug and remembers him peering beneath it, always the curious one. She fingers the weave of a basket like Little Bird might be doing right now, if he were here. And then Adelaide opens her front door and sits on the cabin steps.

The chickens are about, but Adelaide has no words for them today, and she shoos them off. They flutter away from her, but not without one last cursory glance from Henry, letting her know she's become neglect-ful. She nods as though the words were spoken aloud, and then Henry ushers Zelda past the garden.

Adelaide looks to the mound of earth that is now Little Bird.

But Little Bird is not alone.

The wild woman is there, running her hands lightly atop the dirt. Adelaide watches in silence. She should leave them—this moment does not belong to her—but she cannot bear to move.

The wild woman does not scream or snarl. She is collected and doc-ile. It's clear to Adelaide that the wild woman has already experienced death in her young life. Unlike River, this woman is not confused. She knows her boy is not coming back.

The wild woman makes sounds at the earth—a grunt that carries a languishing note at the end, followed by a low thrumming whine which has the feel of a question. Adelaide has spent many nights picking apart the sounds of the Blue Ridge Mountains. Most nights, the sound of the bugs and the trees and the water and the wind all blur together into a feral kind of white noise, one sound indistinguishable from the next. But *these* sounds are something different. These sounds are wild, untamed. They are designed to rise above the cacophony.

Once the wild woman has smoothed the dirt into a fine tapestry, she begins to howl. It is gentle at first, and the hair on Adelaide's neck bristles as she watches the woman on all fours, her back arched, face lifted to the sky.

The wild woman pauses, takes another breath, and once again bays into the night.

A smaller voice joins hers from inside the cabin. Adelaide turns to see River at the window, her little face pressed to the glass, her hair damp and strewn across her cheeks. The child's eyes are angry and fierce, but Adelaide is not afraid. River takes a breath and joins her mother in mourning, their two voices merging into something solid, singular, a structure with doors and walls.

Adelaide knows that if she were ever to describe what happened here, words will surely fail her. And so she will never speak of it. This moment is only for the girls—all three of them.

Adelaide straightens her body, takes a deep breath.

The wild woman howls. River howls.

Adelaide howls.

The next morning, Adelaide wakes beside a slumbering River and strokes the girl's hair. She places her forehead against River's and tucks the blanket around the child before slipping out of bed, out of her cabin, and into the clearing for some fresh air.

Adelaide expected the forest to feel different, look different, but the trees are unchanged, bearing no marks of grief from the night before.

Her throat hurts, and Adelaide marvels at what she has become—a crazy old lady howling into the night. If only Catherine could see her now. Adelaide laughs for just a moment before realizing she will likely never see her daughter, or granddaughter, again. They are ghosts to her now, and Adelaide wonders where she went so wrong. Perhaps she should have learned to howl a long time ago.

The cabin is quiet when she returns, and River stands in the kitchen, still covered in garden dirt from the day before. The butter-yellow knitted cap and the gray elephant lay strewn in her wake.

Adelaide cannot decode the look on the girl's face. Her eyes are dark and bewitching, her hair stringy and wild. It seems River is regressing to her more feral tendencies, as evidenced by her hollow stare, her filthy skin.

"Good morning," Adelaide says to River, but the girl does not answer. "Are you hungry? Yes, I suppose you are."

The thought of breakfast makes her stomach churn, but she must feed the child. She may not be able to console her over the death of her brother, or convince the child to wear clothing, but goddamn it, she can feed her.

Adelaide appraises Catherine's grocery stash. She chooses a bag of apples that are just starting to turn, the honey, some cinnamon, and grabs a cast-iron pan for the fireplace.

As sweet fragrances fill the cabin, Adelaide wonders what she would say to River, if it were even possible. She scoops a small amount of shortening from a jar and drops it into the pan. The apples darken, and the honey melts into a lacquer, the cinnamon blooming into the melting fat like bronze lily pads.

A scratch and a clatter.

A click and a rattle.

Adelaide turns toward the sound and freezes, honey dripping from the spatula and onto her feet.

River stands beside the sofa, shaking the amber bottle of pills.

The room spins and the spatula clatters to the wood floor. A dozen images flash through Adelaide's mind at once, as if they have already happened: River swallowing pills; vomiting, seizing; eyes rolling back in her head; Adelaide screaming, wake up wake up!; River, limp, carried from the cabin; a second mound in the garden beside Little Bird.

And Adelaide, alone. Forever alone.

Adelaide rushes toward River, and the girl shields her face. As much as Adelaide does not want to strike the girl, as much as she simply wants to wrap River in her arms and protect her from every bad thing in this world, the sound of the slap cleaves through the room as Adelaide strikes the pill bottle from River's hand. They stare at each other in stunned silence as the bottle rolls across the floor, little white disks tumbling within.

There are no tears for River. A few for Adelaide. Adelaide smothers her face with one hand and extends the other to River, who recoils against the sofa, baring her teeth.

Adelaide slowly backs away from the child and snatches the pill bottle from the floor. She walks to the kitchen and holds it up to the window, examining the pills in the sunlight. Oh, how she wants the pain to stop. But these pills won't touch the kind of pain Adelaide feels inside. Not anymore.

She looks to River, the tears finally streaming down her scared little face, and Adelaide knows that everything has changed between them. She must make it right because the girl has nobody else.

Adelaide pours the pills into her palm. These pills were to be her exit. Her deliverance. The end to her farmer's life. But everything is different now, and Adelaide is no longer allowed to die.

She drops them two by two into the drain and turns on the faucet.

Tonight, the only thing that moves in the cabin is the fire in the hearth.

River is asleep in the bedroom, but there will be no rest for Adelaide this night, and so she pushes into the sofa, her breath forming a cloud despite the heat from the fireplace.

Adelaide listens to the soft, steady breathing coming from the bedroom. River is okay. For now. And for that, she is grateful.

Adelaide reaches for a match on the side table and lights the small lantern she keeps there. As if in reflection, another much smaller light glows outside her window. It is red, like the cherry glow of a cigarette. Her breath catches in her throat. She and River are not alone.

Through the window, she sees him. The old man with the dark, bewitching eyes. He leans against a tree, smoking a cigarette and watching her cabin. His white shirt glows like a buoy in the waves of a nighttime sea. How long has he been watching her? Was it he who was trailing her from the other side of the frozen river, just yesterday? River at her side. Little Bird in her arms.

What does he know?

Adelaide swallows a boulder, feeling more isolated than ever before. With River under her care, Adelaide's life is no longer one of solitude. But she, alone, must stand for them both. She considers exit routes, hiding spots, potential weaponry. The old man's gaze pierces her like a line of stitches and Adelaide is shocked she didn't notice it earlier.

He does not approach, but he may as well be inside her cabin. Still, he is too close. She trembles not with fear, but with anger. How dare this man. How dare he intimidate her like this? On her own goddamn property. Never again will he step foot in her home.

Adelaide grinds her fists into the sofa and stands. Although he is older now, she is as well, and she stands no better a fight against him this night than she did all those years ago. He had been strong. *So strong.* And he carries that strength with him still. She recognizes it in his hands, his face, his eyes.

She was afraid back then. And she's been afraid ever since. But starting now, in this very moment, she will be afraid of him no longer. She will show the old man strength. Opposition. For River.

And he will come no closer to her cabin.

Adelaide steps out of her front door and into the cold, wrapping her coat tightly around her shoulders.

The old man brings the cigarette to his lips.

Adelaide's mouth is dry, and words do not come. Strength, it seems, is harder to express than to declare. But she wants to be the first to speak. She *must* be the first to speak.

"What do you want?" she manages.

"My boys think you know somethin' 'bout our crops."

The man leans against a tree and crosses his legs. Getting comfortable.

There is quite a distance between them. His words are little more than a whisper but sound carries easily in the forest.

Adelaide snorts. Like she gives a damn about their crops.

"But now I see," he says. "It's not what you *know*. It's what you *got*." The old man spits into the snow.

Adelaide thinks of River, fast asleep, alone in the cabin.

"What I've *got* is none of your business."

The man pauses, smiles, and spreads his arms. "It's all my business."

Adelaide prepares her response, hopes to sound threatening. She speaks low, almost a growl. A little bit feral. "You will not step one foot on this property. Not tonight, not tomorrow, not ever again." Adelaide holds his gaze before adding, "I remember you."

He smiles. Most of his teeth are still intact.

Adelaide feels sick. He's taunting her with his silence.

"I guess mountain lions aren't the only monsters in these woods," she says.

The old man smokes, stares.

Adelaide needs to move this along. He is a trespasser on her land, and she wants him gone. There is nothing left to say. But the old man seems relaxed and in no particular hurry.

"Now speakin' of monsters," he begins, "my boys are damn near convinced you're a witch."

Adelaide counts her breaths to calm her racing heart.

"They say you got some creature in your house. Maybe a wolf, or hell, I don't know."

Adelaide swallows the knot in her throat. Did he take a step closer, or is that her imagination?

The old man flicks his cigarette into the snow. "Yes, ma'am, my boys are damn near 'bout to light the torches and run you right on outta these mountains." He shrugs. "They aren't the brightest. But they're good boys, and they're loyal to their family."

He pauses, waiting for a response. When Adelaide does not speak, he continues. "So now I figure I gotta come down here and see for myself. And what do I see? Tell me *witch*, what did I see last night?"

Adelaide owes him nothing. Less than nothing. A shovel to the skull is what she owes him.

"Honestly, I don't much care 'bout the damage to my crops." He trains his gaze on Adelaide. "Now that I know you're hidin' my kin."

The snow burns Adelaide's eyes. "They are not . . ." She can't even say the words. "They are not . . ."

"I may be old but I ain't senile. One remembers a woman like that. Skinny, pretty enough. Didn't say much." He winks at Adelaide.

Adelaide cannot speak, cannot think. The image of the wild woman, growling, spitting, biting while pinned down by this beast is too much for her to bear. She hopes it is a lie, tells herself it is a lie.

She looks to the old man, her mouth open, her voice mute.

"It's in the eyes," he says.

The old man points to his face and then to the cabin. He smiles, and Adelaide knows the truth of his words. She's seen it herself.

The old man straightens and clears his throat. When he speaks again, his voice is soothing, businesslike. "I'll let you play house a few days more. I'm a reasonable man, and I s'pose you're enjoyin' their company." He takes a long drag off his cigarette, shifting it to the other side of his lips. "But I expect you'll deliver them to me."

The old man removes his hat and wrings it in his hands, as if the breeze has suddenly become warmer, and he no longer needs such protection.

Them. He doesn't know about Little Bird's death, and she won't correct him. He doesn't get to know.

"I will do no such thing. Get off my property," she says, barely a whisper, her conviction slowing. "Get off my goddamn property."

"I'll give you one week, witch. One week to get 'em cleaned up and ready. And put some clothes on 'em fergodsake. Goddamn animals. And if you don't deliver 'em by then, I'll come for 'em myself. You won't like it."

"They're just children." Adelaide wraps her coat tightly around herself as though it is armor.

"*My* children, you best remember. Pretty little girls, ain't they?"

Adelaide is frozen, unable to step forward and rush toward him, unable to step back inside her cabin.

"One week, witch." And he points at her to make it so. "One week from tonight."

The old man smiles, and Adelaide nearly collapses.

"And *now*," he says with a flourish, "I will get off your goddamn property."

Adelaide stands at her door until he's walked back to a car she hadn't seen parked by the road. She stands there until the taillights disappear behind the trees. She stands there until she can no longer tolerate being so far away from River. And then she rushes inside, bolts the door, and lodges a chair beneath the handle.

18

The old man's words have etched a ravine into Adelaide's brain. She is rattled, undone, and even attempting breakfast proves too difficult this morning. She worries for River. Adelaide couldn't protect *herself* from this man all those years ago, and now she must find a way to protect them both.

They have sat like this for a while—Adelaide and River, side by side on the floor, their backs to the sofa. One gray bun coming loose from its clip. One dark mane of curls vibrating with every trembling breath. A barrier of uncertainty has formed between them. Doubt has crept in. It's been like this since the pill incident.

It took awhile for Adelaide to lure the girl closer. She began with pieces of beef jerky from Catherine's grocery stash. When the meat didn't work, Adelaide resorted to a spoonful of peanut butter, which should have been her first guess all along, as River slowly made her way across the living room, skirting the edge of the rug like a cliff's edge.

And when Adelaide patted the floor beside her, River obeyed. A glorious victory.

And so here they sit, two girls licking peanut butter from spoons. Morning light streams through the small window by the door, and though not much can be seen from this angle, Adelaide knows it isn't snowing.

She reaches for River's hand, but the girl pulls away.

Okay, Adelaide thinks, I deserve that.

"You aren't my only little girl, you know," Adelaide states with the rise of an eyebrow. "That woman who was here last week—that's *my* little girl. And she brought *her* little girl."

River listens, tilting her ear and seeking more. Adelaide wonders how many words the girl understands. She wonders what the girl could say if she tried.

Adelaide fluffs out her hair, and it lies heavily across her shoulders. She doesn't know if she should continue this discussion with River. Some topics aren't appropriate for children. But it feels good to talk to somebody. She could use the distraction. Besides, River doesn't understand, anyway.

Adelaide takes a breath so deep her chest hurts and prepares to say the one thing she has never allowed herself to admit.

"I fear I never truly loved my daughter."

Adelaide peers at River to gauge a response, but there is none, so she continues.

"If I loved her, I wouldn't have been relieved when she left, right? I would've chased her down, begged her to stay. But god, she hated me, hated this place, this life. And when she left, a weight was lifted from my shoulders, even though I was angry at her for leaving. I just read her letter, over and over, grateful that it was finally done."

Adelaide shakes her head, hates herself for speaking the words aloud.

"Of course I loved her," she corrects. "I shouldn't have said that. We never understood each other is all. We are a different breed, me and Catherine."

River does not respond, but she does hiccup, and somehow that is enough.

"You don't understand what I'm saying, yet I keep talking. And then I feel foolish for saying more."

Adelaide feels River's small hand on her knee. Somehow, this mute, feral child understands her better than her own blood. She places her hand over River's and squeezes it.

"You know, little one, I thought I'd been alone in this valley all these years, but you were out there all along, weren't you?"

Adelaide moves her hand to River's head, mussing her unruly hair, and hopes the girl won't pull away. She doesn't. Adelaide curls a lock around her finger, and River inches closer.

"There is a bad man in these woods, River. An evil man. He thinks you belong to him. And in a way, I suppose you do, and I'm sorry for that. How your mother kept you two safe, I do not know. And now I've failed you both—you *and* your brother—and I don't know how to live with that. He's coming for you, little one, and we don't have much more time together. I don't know how to protect you, and it just breaks my heart."

The silence stretches on for the longest of moments before River finally speaks. But when she does, the language of her feral tongue floods from the girl's mouth. Adelaide nearly shrieks with surprise.

Just as River does not understand Adelaide, neither can Adelaide understand River. But she listens to the girl's sounds, and the lilts in her speech, and the change of tones near the end of her sentences as River carries on, word after mysterious word.

There is anger in the child, but also laughter, and though the girl speaks of things Adelaide cannot know, she is grateful for the exchange.

When River points to the kitchen window, Adelaide knows she speaks of Little Bird, and she listens for clues to the girl's understanding. River speaks softly, with a touch of resignation, and she knows the girl does not blame her.

Like an opera, River sings—telling nothing but giving away everything. Adelaide feels the vowels and the consonants and the squeaks and the chirps somewhere deep in her heart. Somewhere she hasn't accessed in a very long time. The last time she felt this way was as a young woman with a swollen belly, knitting a butter-yellow cap that could be for either a little boy or a little girl. Adelaide felt many things back then, before it all became too difficult. Before she began to expect hardship. The days when every morning brought new blessings, and old age existed in some parallel universe she would never know.

As River expresses her feelings in a secret language, Adelaide closes her eyes and listens to the child unburden herself. And for the briefest of moments, uncertainty and fear also exist in some parallel universe they will never know.

The following day brings a moist chill to the air that is as merciless as the old man's words. If Adelaide were a warrior, she would plan for battle. If she were a king, she would rally her soldiers. But Adelaide is neither of these things—she is an old woman. She holds a child, not a weapon.

And she has already lost a day.

A thud at the front door startles Adelaide.

Not yet.

Adelaide sprints to the living room window, knowing that if someone is on her steps, her presence will be self-confessed. She sees nothing but ignorance is no longer an option. Adelaide snatches a knife from the kitchen, grips the hilt, grips the doorknob, grips her nerves, and pushes open the door.

A small breeze rushes past her and flutters the curtains. There are no men outside her cabin door. And no wild woman. But there is something at her feet.

Nearly camouflaged against the hazel wood of her front step are four small, yellow eggs the size of beechnut seeds. One has cracked, thick fluid seeping from a jagged fissure.

Adelaide is reminded of the cats her family owned when she was a girl. They would often bring small dead animals into the home—lizards, mice, cockroaches. Her mother assured her that they were gifts of love, even if unwanted.

Adelaide doesn't recognize the kind of eggs she holds in her hands, but she does know one thing for sure—they are gifts.

But gift or not, something about the eggs bothers Adelaide. A bad omen written in spilled yolk.

She should be more optimistic. The wild woman has left a peace offering, and this could be the beginning of a partnership, should Adelaide be so bold to assume. Perhaps in the enemy of her enemy, she could find an ally.

Adelaide peers into the barren trees beyond her property line, and smiles.

"Thank you," she whispers, grateful for her unexpected friend.

After a breakfast of scrambled eggs, Adelaide sits on the couch beside River, brushing the girl's long, curly hair.

She tries to feel the old man, somewhere in the woods. In *her* woods. She wants to believe that he will not come early. But she knows better than anyone that his word cannot be trusted.

Where are you? How can I stop you? When will you be here?

The clock ticks loudly from Adelaide's bedroom, echoing through the small cabin like a fist upon her door, her windows. *Soon-soon-soon.*

Beside her, River grows sleepy, and once the child's breathing becomes slow and steady, Adelaide leaves the girl on the sofa to nap, and retreats from her cabin. Far away from the ticking clock.

She gathers her hair into a bun at the nape of her neck as snow dusts her shoulders, and she gazes across the landscape, relieved to find no men on her property. Yet.

She circles her cabin with hesitant steps. This will be the first time since Little Bird's burial that Adelaide has entered the garden. She doesn't know if her heart can bear it, but she can delay no more—it is time to visit her son. While she still can.

Her garden is no longer a garden. It is a graveyard, and the very earth beneath her feet seems to have changed to reflect its new state. The sky is darker, too, as though the sun has granted a reprieve.

Adelaide had intended to sit by Little Bird, speak to him, apologize, cry. Howl. *Anything.* But she is not ready. Perhaps she never will be, and she will avoid the garden forever, like a secret buried beneath a floorboard.

Adelaide dawdles among the planters, appraising what remains of her beloved garden. The weeds have become brown and stringy, and Adelaide uproots a handful, tossing them over the fence. Little Bird deserves more respect than this, and Adelaide rips out every weed she can find. She clears fallen branches and splintered willow, and is planning where she will plant flowers for Little Bird come spring when she trips over something concealed in the dirt—a steel rod that once secured the trap that nearly killed his mother.

She'd buried the trap itself, but the rod is still lodged in the dirt, mocking her, impaled in the ground beside her Little Bird. Adelaide can think of nothing more cruel.

Adelaide loosens the rod and skirts the fence until she is outside of it, standing before the mound of dirt that conceals the trap itself. She doesn't want to see it, doesn't want to touch it, but Adelaide must rid her conscience of this awful thing once and for all.

She claws at the ground with her fingers, tossing dirt and leaves behind her like a hound unearthing a burrow, until the trap crowns through the soil with one final tug.

Adelaide gathers the trap, chain, and rod into her skirt, and she stands. The air is warm today despite the morning snowfall, and if the river has thawed, it will all sink to the silty bottom, swallowed forever. She walks faster, impatient for the water, eager for the splash.

But when Adelaide arrives, the river is still frozen solid. This will not do. Suddenly the warm air feels like a lie, and she curses the sky.

There is only one place to hide it, and she shudders to think of it there, in her home. But there is no other way.

Adelaide hauls the trap back to her cabin. She will hide it under the floorboard that pulls away from the nails, until the ice thaws, and then she will chuck it into the center of the river.

Adelaide steps gingerly across the living room with the contraption in her arms, careful not to wake River.

She circles the sofa and kneels behind it, wedging her fingertip beneath the floorboard that pulls away from the nails. The opening beneath is dark and thick with shadow. For years, this one floorboard hid the most sentimental and regretful secrets of her past.

And now, its black, cavernous hole will hide just one more.

Adelaide lowers the trap into the space below, slips the chain and rod beside it, and replaces the board. She then stands and pulls the sofa toward her, watching the floorboard—and its final secret—vanish beneath the frame. And just like that, the trap disappears as if it's not even there.

Roused by the motion, River sits up and looks around, laughing at Adelaide. It seems she has enjoyed the ride.

In another life, Adelaide would take the child to a playground, push her on a swing set. She would teach River to throw her legs forward and shift her weight and sail high into the air. Wouldn't that be something? That's how it would be. If Adelaide were a different woman. And River were a different child. And this were another place altogether.

PART 3
MEN

PART 3

MEN

19

The sun has melted all but the most stubborn snow, and as Adelaide stares out the kitchen window, she wonders how long a reprieve she's been granted.

She wraps an apron around her hips and fills the pocket with the last few days' worth of food scraps. The chickens will be pleased. But Henry and Zelda are not the only reason for her visit to the kitchen.

Adelaide opens her cutlery drawer and surveys the weaponry. If an old lady needs to carry a knife in order to protect her family, so be it. Adelaide grabs a large, dangerous blade, but it is too unwieldy in her grip, and she returns it to the drawer. Below a few dull butter knives and a potato peeler, she finds it. The paring knife—slim blade, curved at the end. Rarely used, and still very sharp. Small enough to hold, but angled in the right way, she could do some damage. Yes, this is the one, and she drops it into her pocket.

Adelaide leaves River to a breakfast of griddle cakes, and she walks into the afternoon. Henry and Zelda rush toward her, clucking at her feet, and she disperses chunks of apple and bread onto the ground. The chickens chortle their gratitude.

Adelaide peers around the trees but sees nothing, hears nothing. Still, she is tense and ready, and she grips the knife handle tucked inside her apron pocket. Even something as rudimentary as feeding the chickens now feels a bit precarious.

Adelaide needs to figure out how to handle the old man. She must prepare. Because it's going to take more than piss and mousetraps to protect River.

She will not wait in limbo for men to decide her and River's fate. For men to come. For men to take. Adelaide will have to make an offensive move in order to win this battle with the old man. She *must* strike first.

The tip of the blade cuts into Adelaide's finger, and she winces, wiping the blood onto her apron. She reminds herself that if she is strong enough to make life, she is strong enough to take it away. Maybe that's why she is on this earth—to protect River, no matter what. Maybe that's why she took a pocket full of pills to the river only to find herself in her cabin that evening with nothing more than a hangover.

The sun warms Adelaide's skin. Her feet are warm, and her heart is warm, and it feels like a blessing. The forest is once again on her side.

Tonight, when the sun goes down, and River is asleep, Adelaide will go to the farm. She could walk there in an hour's time, give or take. She hopes the weather holds.

As Adelaide returns to her cabin, she traces her bleeding finger across her apron, like the chalk outline of a body.

Adelaide grasps her tea which has already cooled on the table. Sips it. Thinks of the old man.

She doesn't know his name. She's never been able to quantify him with vowels and consonants. He exists to her only as a presence, the stain of a memory she's tried to forget. It is no less true today than all those years ago.

Adelaide feels the passage of time like a wound, gashes lashed across her skin.

She's tired of waiting. But the sun is still high in the sky and she forces herself to calm down. She wants to go. Now. Before they come to her instead.

Before she chickens out.

Adelaide can't remember the last time she was this warm in the middle of winter, sweating, her breath like a sandstorm whorling in and out of her lungs.

She listens to her clock, echoing from her bedroom wall. *Tick-tick-tick.* Today, the clock is the voice of better judgment, whispering, *wait-wait-wait.*

Adelaide stands outside her cabin in the dark. The night is quiet, and though a chill has settled in her bones, no snow fell this evening. This will make her trek easier. The house keys jangle in her hand as she locks the dead bolt from the outside—another new thing she has become accustomed to over the previous weeks.

She wears a housedress, her heaviest coat, and the apron. Of course, the apron. And in the apron pocket, she has her paring knife and a box of matches to keep lit the oil lantern she carries.

One step outside her door is all that is needed now, and then she will be on her way to the farm. But Adelaide has no idea what she is going to do when she arrives. She is an old lady. What harm could she possibly do to these men? She has a knife in her apron pocket designed for slicing fruit, not throats. She has no gun, not even a bow and arrow. And she carries an oil lantern, *forgodsake.* She's practically a cavewoman. But primitive tools or not, she can sit and wait no longer. She must try. If she can sneak up behind one of the men (*boys*, really), maybe she can take them out, one at a time. She's hunted before. This is no different. *No different.* If given the opportunity, she must do it quickly and quietly, before they can cry out for help.

One at a time.

Something moves through the trees. Are the men here already?

Dear god, they know, and they are here already.

Adelaide's heart is a drum line across her chest as she watches the figure, merely a black shadow slipping through the darkness of a nearly moonless night. And then the shadow halts, stands, and Adelaide is breathless as her eyes adjust to the gloom.

The wild woman stands at the edge of the tree line. Adelaide has never before seen the woman upright, was unsure it was even possible. But here she is, elegant, thin, and much taller than Adelaide imagined. More beautiful, too. A relic better suited to a natural history museum than the Blue Ridge Mountains.

The long, muscular body of the wild woman pulses with each breath she takes. There is something different about the wild woman—she stands at attention, mere yards from Adelaide, not even a hint of malice in her eyes.

Tonight, the wild woman is no beast. She is simply a woman, a mother. And together, beneath a dark and barren sky, the two women acknowledge each other as allies.

Adelaide walks cautiously toward the edge of her property and turns, fearful she has misread the situation, and the wild woman will be on her heels, teeth bared and ready. But Adelaide has nothing to fear from the wild woman this night. She stands guard beside the cabin, obscured beneath the shadow of the eaves. For the very first time, Adelaide is comfortable leaving River alone. No harm will come to the girl as she sleeps. Not tonight. And for the first time in many years—decades, even—Adelaide has a friend.

Adelaide stands just outside the property line of the old man's farm and places her lantern upon the ground to avoid being seen. In her fist, she grips the paring knife. It has been in her hand for the last hour of her trek, and her knuckles are stiff and strained. She stretches her fingers as she waits for her heart rate to slow.

Adelaide's knees hurt and her shins are scraped. She took a hard fall near the end of a dirt road, nearly losing her oil lantern in the process. She shudders to think of a trek back to her cabin, devoid of light.

She surveys the land, expecting sentries, guard posts, men with guns and high beams, that sort of thing. What she finds instead is a dilapidated trailer, a few parked vehicles, and ceaseless rows of plants. Some have succumbed to the winter, while others still hang on, radiating green, yellow, purple. She knows the smell. On a summer's day, the scent drifts all the way down into her valley. But now, at the beginning of winter, the smell is already dusty, old. It is still strong enough, however, to be in her throat, on her tongue; she can taste it.

A chain-link fence safeguards the crops, and she follows its length toward the trailer, slinking through the darkness like the mountain cat she tried to trap in her garden a month ago, more like a lifetime ago. The lights are on in the trailer. Figures pass by the window.

Adelaide marvels that she has gotten so close without detection, but then wonders if there is a man in a tree, or on the roof, watching her advance, waiting for her to get closer, closer, *closer*. She would be a fool to assume she's gotten away with anything at all.

Adelaide steps on a fallen branch, and when it snaps, the sound echoes across the field. From inside the trailer, a dog barks, and Adelaide ducks toward the ground, smothering the lantern.

She holds her breath.

Adelaide doesn't belong here. This is madness.

She takes a slow and steady step backward, disappearing into the trees. She retraces her steps down the length of the fence, gingerly, as if every move she makes has the potential to rain tragedy down upon her.

By the time she approaches the front of the men's property, she is at a trot, every cell in her body begging to run fast and far away from this place.

Adelaide steadies herself against the fence post, gasping for breath and struggling to stay upright. She surveys the land, the trailer in the distance, the bordering trees, the chain-link fence, and the field of plants, many still raging against the end of the growing season.

She wants to hurt the old man, like he hurt her. She wants to take something away from him. Her attack plan may have been reckless and impulsive, but her retreat was equally rash. She must do *something*.

Adelaide plunges her hand into the apron, trading her knife for matches. The sulfur ignites, and Adelaide brings the matchstick down onto the first plant she can reach over the fence. The leaves curl beneath the heat, brown from the fire.

And the flame goes out.

She lights another match and holds it to the plant.

"C'mon, c'mon," she whispers to the flame.

The leaf smolders before the cold and damp snuff this one out as well.

Adelaide curses beneath her breath and lights a third match. There aren't many left in the box, and she protects this little flame with her palm, willing the plant to burst into flame, send fire and maelstrom through the fields, engulf the trailer and the men inside. There may have been no snow this evening, but there is plenty of moisture, and the flame struggles to stay aglow as she waves it beneath the tip of the leaves.

In the distance, a door slams and two men step onto the porch. Adelaide hunkers below the plant line, rising just high enough to see their heads. It is the brothers—those two young men that seem to ricochet from each other in opposite directions. They each light a cigarette and then share a laugh before one places his hand on the other's chest, pushing him back. He smells the air and peers across the fields.

Adelaide panics, and blows out the small flame that has erupted on the end of a leaf, fanning the air as she peeks over the plants once more. The young man reaches for something on the porch, taking it in his hands.

A shotgun. He lifts the weapon to his shoulder, scanning the fields.

Adelaide's chest constricts, and for a moment, she fears she may never breathe again. What will she do if they see her? What *can* she do? She feels stupid now—*so stupid*—for ever coming here in the first place. She wants to run back to her home. Back to River asleep in the cabin. Back to safety. But if she runs now, they will see her for sure.

"Hey!" His voice echoes through the still of the night. A blast rings through the sky as the man fires a warning shot.

The hounds erupt from inside the trailer.

Adelaide steadies her nerves and stands erect before their field. Tonight, she will let them know she is not easy prey. She is a force. A goddamned feral beast.

She strikes a remaining match and holds it to the lantern wick.

So many sounds at once. Shouting, doors slamming, men running, dogs barking.

Adelaide can't think. She can't see anything before her. All she sees is River. The child will suffer because of her. Because of her failure. Dear god, she's done it again. The lantern swings in her hand, casting twisting shadows across the landscape, as she pitches the lantern into the center of the field.

It erupts.

Fiery oil coats plants, soil, fence. The shouts of the men turn from anger to panic as the scent of burning foliage fills the night air. They are coming for her and she needs to run. Now. *Now. NOW!*

Adelaide runs down the dirt road, blinded by fire and terror, and into the darkness.

It is nearly morning by the time Adelaide collapses onto her front step. Though her return home was slow and humbling without her lantern, she gasps as though she has run a marathon. In her mind, she saw herself attacked by dogs, run down by trucks, fired upon at every turn.

Her clothes, which last night were shades of peach, are now stained beyond recognition. Her skirt is muddied, her shoes soaked black.

The early morning is remarkably silent. Not even a branch groans in the breeze.

Adelaide scans the shadows for evidence of the wild woman, but it seems she has abandoned her post.

As Adelaide unlocks the door with a clatter and enters the stillness of her home, she is consumed by a feeling of safety and protection that she immediately recognizes as false. These walls protect *nothing*. Mere hours ago, she set fire to a field, and the men are probably hunting her down right now. Yet she is in her home, and nothing is amiss. She smells her fingertips to make sure it was not a dream. The scent of smoke reveals everything.

It is darkest in her bedroom, farthest from the glowing embers of the fireplace. Adelaide halts in the doorway. Her bed is empty.

She scans the room and finds River on the floor, tucked into the corner beneath the window, forehead pressed against the glass. She is fast asleep, snoring a slow, child's breath.

Adelaide smiles and creeps closer to the girl, wondering if she could scoop her up and move her back to the bed without waking her. Adelaide reaches for her, angling her hands toward the child's waist when she sees something outside the window. Just beyond River, the wild woman sleeps as well.

Forehead pressed against the glass.

The wild woman hadn't abandoned her daughter—she had *found* her.

Adelaide feels like an intruder in her very own bedroom, and a knot tangles in her throat. She is the keeper of the glass barrier that separates them. Little more than a monster. But River is better off on *this* side of the window. The safe side. She must not lose sight of that.

Adelaide curls up on her sofa, nearest to the fireplace, and warms her hands against the heat. She tucks a pillow beneath her head, beating it into a malleable shape, and she listens for tires, voices, dogs. But sleep takes her fast, and she is not awake when the light of a new day pours through her window.

This morning, there are more gifts at Adelaide's front door. The wild woman is nowhere in sight, left no sound and no footprint. But she left breakfast. This morning, a young red fox, its neck torn out, blood staining the wood of her step.

A terrible sight. Adelaide groans, hangs her head. She aches to think of its grieving mother in the woods.

But Adelaide does not wish to offend the wild woman, nor allow the meat to turn to rot. So she skins and debones, and she and River feast in the stillness of the morning.

After breakfast, the girl grows restless, clawing at the windows, barking commands at Adelaide. When Adelaide takes her to the garden and cleans the debris from Little Bird's grave, she hopes the girl might be curious, or grateful for the outing. But she is neither of these things. She chirps into the forest, running from tree to tree. When that is not enough, the girl drops to her hands and feet, galloping from one corner of the garden to the other. Adelaide is convinced the child might dash into the woods, never to be seen again. And for a moment (just a small moment), Adelaide wishes she would. She cannot keep River safe. Especially now, after torching the old man's farm. Thanks to her, the men could be here at any moment. She wants to tell River to run while she still can. Back to her real mother.

But despite herself, Adelaide slowly approaches the galloping child, and is relieved when River allows herself to be carried into the cabin. And though she does not resist, the wail she leaves in their wake rattles Adelaide throughout the rest of the afternoon.

Tonight, Adelaide retrieves a spare lantern from the kitchen cupboard and fills it with oil. She lights it, and places it on the side table by the sofa. When she sits, River tucks into Adelaide's chest, and she wraps her arm around the little girl—*her* little girl—as together they watch the fireplace.

Adelaide plucks a few leaves from River's hair, letting them fall to the floor. She tries to memorize the girl's face. Her dark, bewitching eyes. Every strand of her mane. Her knees, which poke from her spindly legs like apples on a stick. Adelaide doesn't know why the girl suddenly looks up at her and smiles, but she takes it as an opportunity to memorize the dimple just beside her lip, the glisten of her eyes, the fuzz on her jawline, haloed by the flames.

Adelaide smells River's hair, the side of her face, taking the scent into her lungs. Today, for just a moment, she had hoped the girl would run away, but Adelaide is glad she did not.

The cabin shakes, and the canopies whistle, and Adelaide tells herself it is only the wind. Something bangs against the roof, and she tells herself it is only a fallen branch. Because it has to be. She is not yet ready for anything else.

The clock ticks from the bedroom, echoing through the cabin. *Tick-tick-tick.*

Men-men-men.

She hugs River closer.

A flash of light fills her window, and Adelaide holds her breath before hearing the distant roll of thunder. Lightning. Only lightning.

Beneath the sofa, under the floorboard that pulls away from the nails, the trap rattles and clangs against its chain, the sound echoing through the small cabin.

Adelaide cannot allow River to fall into the hands of the men. She won't see that happen, not while there is still breath in her lungs. But if she were to release the girl back to the wild, back to her feral mother, what kind of life awaits her in the wilderness? Hardship. Danger. She thinks of River outside, sleeping in the dirt, rain soaking her until she is shivering, wondering why Adelaide no longer loves her.

No. She won't allow it.

Adelaide thinks of the red fox, dead on her doorstep. Was it a threat from the wild woman? Will Adelaide's throat meet the same fate?

She worries they are no longer allies. Perhaps it was all a trick so that Adelaide would lower her guard. Perhaps their truce came with a time limit, and Adelaide has delayed too long. Perhaps there was never a truce at all. The fox was a bad omen. The second one in days.

Adelaide doesn't know what the wild woman has planned, if anything. But she knows one thing for sure—the men will soon be here. When she torched the old man's farm, she made her choice, and she must accept whatever comes next. If this is her last night with River, it will have all been worth it. Because right now—finally—the child is hers.

20

The girl wakes and looks around. It is dark. She can barely see the fire. But she can smell it, and she knows that even though it is not big, it will still hurt her if she were to get too close. She touched it once, many moons ago. A piece of tree glowing like the sun. The girl rubs her fingers together now. She can still feel the hurt if she tries really hard. Maybe that is why she is awake.

She begins to sit up but cannot move. The woman's arms are tight around her. They hold her down. The girl fears for a moment that she cannot breathe and will end up under the ground in the square forest next to brother, but then she breathes and knows she is okay. Mother used to hold her like this. And brother, too. Mother held the girl and brother at the same time. The girl wishes they could all sleep together now, but she knows that they can't because mother is not here, and brother is not here. But the woman is here, and the warm, soggy hugs don't feel so bad.

Sometimes, the girl sees mother outside. Mother is running again. She is very strong and very fast again, and mother wants her back. The girl could've left this morning. She could've run away from the woman. But she didn't see mother anywhere. Salty tears drip down her cheek and pool in her ear. The girl misses mother. Maybe that is why she is awake.

The girl wants to practice saying words, like she and brother used to do in the sleep cave, late at night. But brother is not here to practice with her. Brother is not here to smile when she gets a word right or laugh when she gets it wrong. Brother is nowhere now, and the girl is alone. So she practices the words they learned, all by herself.

"Sheet," she whispers, breath barely passing her teeth.

"Food."

"No."

"Fire." That one was hard for her to say at first, but brother helped her.

"Chic-ken." That word is a hard one, too. Like it's two words. The girl had to learn them separately and then put them together in her mind. But she still says each piece, one at a time.

"Dead." Brother was not here to practice this one with the girl. She learned it on her own, when the woman became very sad and screamed this word over and over.

The girl feels something that she doesn't recognize, deep in her tummy. It's a little like being sick, and a little like being dizzy and a little like all her insides have come out through a hole in her chest, and she is nothing but empty skin. She feels like she wants to laugh, and like she wants to cry, and like she wants to scream as loud as she can. Like the time she, mother, and brother were scaring hares from a hole. They screamed and screamed and hit the dirt and stomped their feet and made all kinds of scary and silly noises together. That's the feeling. That's what she wants to do right now. For brother. She wants to go outside and stomp her feet and make all kinds of scary and silly noises so brother will come out of the hole. But the girl understands more than she used to. Brother isn't hiding in a hole like a hare. He's dead. He got very sick, like she was sick when she ate the pointy flowers. But unlike her, brother didn't get better, and he went away forever, and he's never coming back, no matter how hard the girl stomps on the dirt. Maybe that is why she is awake.

The woman squeezes tighter, and the girl feels the woman's hurt. The woman is hurting so deeply that the girl thinks her own chest might burst open, and she wraps her thin arms around her belly to keep everything inside. She hopes she is strong enough. The hurt is in her teeth, and the hurt is in her gut, and the girl did not realize that one person could have so much hurt. Maybe that is why she is awake.

The girl shifts and stretches and wraps the woman's arms tightly around her so she can be warm and wet again, just like with mother and brother. If she closes her eyes really tight and thinks really hard, she can feel the roughness of mother's hands touching her. She can smell brother's hair right in front of her face. She can hear brother mumble in his sleep, and hear birds above, and feel the wind blowing through the trees.

The girl does not want to open her eyes for the rest of the night, because right now, she is no longer in the cabin. She is in the forest with her family. And if she opens her eyes, it will all go away.

Adelaide wakes with the taste of vomit on her tongue. The rising sun is like a sickness, and her body moves as though constructed of crooked lumber and rusted screws. Already she is sweating. If it were summer, she would blame the heat. But it is not summer.

Last night was silent. No men. Adelaide had not expected a restful night's sleep, and their lack of retaliation is unsettling. They're toying with her, allowing her to grow complacent. Adelaide presses her knuckles into her eyes, swallows the lump in her throat.

Her nightgown is discolored with a dark wetness, and she plucks the fabric from her body to inspect it. Sweat. Dirt. A stain the size of a small child.

River.

Dear god, River.

Adelaide leaps from the sofa and barks, "River, River, River."

She bolts from room to room, searching corners she's already searched. There are not many places to hide in her cabin, and she paces back and forth, hoping to see something she missed. Under the bed, above the cupboards, in the closet, behind the coats and slippers.

She sees it then—a sliver of sunlight from beneath the open front door. A gust of wind pushes the door farther open, flinging dirt and snow into the living room.

The lock has not been broken. It is simply unlatched.

Adelaide failed to lock the cabin door last night and they have come, after all. The men. They have her. Took her from the sofa while Adelaide slept. Snatched the child right from her lap, and she has no one to blame but herself.

Adelaide rushes to the door and crashes into it, her shoulder exploding against the wood as she emerges blind into the brilliant daylight.

No tire tracks. No hounds. No sign of the men.

Or River.

Adelaide doesn't know where to run, where to look. But she hears a noise and launches into flight, flinging herself toward *something*, because anything is better than the fear. The not-knowing.

And then she sees River.

Behind the wattle fence, beyond the garden that once had a gate, River sits and talks to her brother.

Adelaide walks quietly, avoids branches, controls her breathing. She doesn't want to intrude—not really—but neither can she stanch her curiosity. As she creeps closer to River, she hears that familiar, special-speak of the children.

River turns and their eyes meet. Adelaide's presence doesn't seem to bother her, and so Adelaide sits, knee to knee, beside the girl.

But River, it seems, has no more to say, and the two of them sit in silence.

Adelaide runs a hand across Little Bird's grave, smoothing the dirt. She looks for Henry and Zelda, but they are nowhere to be found.

How different her life is now. A month ago, Adelaide was the only person in the Blue Ridge Mountains. This was never the case, of course, though she may as well have been. But she'd been wrong. She'd been wrong about so many things. She knows this now. So here she sits, in her garden.

With a daughter.

And a dead son.

Moffit gone, Henry and Zelda now all alone.

A wild woman stalking her home.

Evil men at her doorstep.

River's hand glides toward Adelaide, and something dangles from the girl's fingers. Adelaide jumps. In the girl's tiny hand, a dead snake. In her other hand, a second, its head snapped nearly in two. Adelaide corrects her scowl and takes the offering.

River smiles, and as Adelaide examines the snake in her hand, River begins to chew flesh from the one in hers.

Adelaide scans the forest, looking for the wild woman. She has been here. And once again, she has brought gifts. But there are no signs of her. No footprints, no sound, no feel of her in the morning air.

The child has collected her own.

Adelaide wants to smack the snake from the girl's hand and launch it into the trees, but she hesitates. River may as well be eating a summer sausage. At the end of the day, it is simply food, so she lets the child be.

In the distance, a sound that has become all too familiar. Subtle at first but growing louder. Snapping branches and rustling leaves. Someone approaches. Closer to the cabin. Closer to River.

The very air, it seems, is committed to snatching everything from Adelaide's life. Perhaps this is her penance for wanting more, for wanting a second chance. Not everyone gets a second chance. Not everyone deserves it.

She lifts River from her knees and pulls her toward the cabin. The child protests but is no match for Adelaide, old woman or not.

At the cabin door, Adelaide pushes River into the living room and turns to scan the forest.

Tucked within the tree line, just outside the wattle fence, Adelaide spots the wild woman, nearly invisible in the shadows.

River presses against Adelaide's legs, craning to see into the clearing, but Adelaide drives the girl back, thrusting her toward the sofa.

Adelaide still holds the dead snake in her hand—her third bad omen—and she flings the carcass from her fingers, tossing it to the dirt. It lands with a wet thud, and Henry nudges forward to investigate. He fluffs his feathers and pecks at the dead animal until it is skewered by his beak.

Henry chortles a sound of celebration and darts behind the cabin as Adelaide steps inside and locks the door.

For the last hour, the wild woman has stalked the perimeter of Adelaide's property. Her slight limp, though noticeable, does not impede her stealth. Nor her frustration. Adelaide watches from behind the relative safety of her kitchen window, convinced that they are no longer friends.

The wild woman bays, spits, and stomps through half-frozen mud. Sometimes she walks upright, and Adelaide sees her as a woman. At other times she gallops on all fours, and Adelaide sees her as a beast.

This morning, while sitting with River in the garden, Adelaide had a thought. It was fleeting at first and just as quickly dismissed. But the thought persisted, and Adelaide now knows what must be done. For the first time in days, she has a real plan to keep River safe. From men, from beasts, even from Adelaide herself. A mother's ultimate sacrifice. Maybe this time—finally—she's made the right decision.

Adelaide searches the cabin for a basket and finds one above the cupboards, where Little Bird and River once hid before they earned their names. Inside the basket, she places boxes of food, cans of food, and a large canteen of water. She places the butter-yellow knitted cap, the small gray elephant, and a soft, thin blanket into the basket as well, tucking them around the edges so nothing will fall out.

Outside, the wild woman howls, and River flinches.

Outside, the wild woman whines, and River leaps up and down at the window.

Adelaide visits the closet one more time, searching for clothes for River. Though it is too large for a child, Adelaide decides on a shrunken wool shirt. Something she can easily toss over the girl and tie around her waist before she realizes what is happening. The journey ahead of them is too long, and too cold, for a naked child to endure.

Adelaide slips her paring knife into her apron pocket and lays the larger knife on the side table beside the lantern. She then sits next to the girl, placing the basket between them. River reaches for the elephant and Adelaide allows her to pull it out and cuddle it to her chest. The girl rocks back and forth, the animal squished against her belly. With growing apprehension, Adelaide places a hand on River's back.

"I don't know if you can understand me, little one. I suspect you understand more than I give you credit for. Oh dear, how do I explain this?"

River watches her intently.

"Down the mountain," Adelaide begins and pauses, searching for the right words. "Down the mountain, there is a town." She waits for any sign of recognition before continuing, but as usual, River's face is placid. "And that is where people live."

River points to the sofa.

"Yes, *we* live here, but this is not a town. A town is where *lots* of people live. All together. Like a family."

River points out the living room window. To the last place she saw her mother.

"Yes, some people live out there, I suppose, but that's not a town either. And it isn't safe."

Adelaide is failing at this, and she tries to explain it another way.

"Imagine that there are many Adelaides and many Rivers living all around us every day."

Adelaide holds both hands in the air, unfolding her fingers one by one. River's eyes grow wide.

"Yes! Yes, exactly. That's a town. Sort of."

Adelaide rubs her forehead. How is she going to say this? River speaks before she has figured it out.

"Tow . . ."

Adelaide gasps. "Oh my, yes! Town!"

"Tow . . . n."

Adelaide lunges across the sofa and wraps her arms around the girl. River laughs and squeezes back. Adelaide pulls away and grasps her shoulders, staring into those dark, bewitching eyes.

"You did it! Town!"

River smiles and shrugs. A piece of Adelaide's heart breaks away, and she knows it will never grow back. Not after today.

"Wait," she says to River, "I almost forgot."

Adelaide searches the side table, her bedroom dresser, and every drawer and cabinet in her kitchen until she finds it. A scrap of paper bearing the name and address of a stranger. When Adelaide walks back to the sofa, she is slower than before. Because now it's real. And her confidence is quickly draining away.

She sits beside River and shows her the paper.

"This person is a friend of my daughter's. Maybe she will help us. Maybe you can live with her and be a part of her family. Or maybe she can help find you a new family. A family who has been waiting for a little girl, just like you."

River points to the living room window. Her finger is rigid and lean muscles strain in her arm.

"I know. Trust me, I know." Adelaide folds the note and tucks it into the basket. "She's a stranger to you. She's a stranger to me, too. But she's the only person I know, now that Catherine is gone."

She places her hand on the girl's outstretched arm, bringing it down into her lap.

"Out there? Not safe for you. Or for me. Hurt. Pain. In the town, you will have a family. A *real* family. You will have your own bed, and you can go to school and see a doctor when you get sick, and never, ever, *ever*, end up in the ground like Little Bird."

The girl is quiet, and an emotion that looks a little like anger passes over her face but is gone so quickly that Adelaide cannot be sure that it was there at all. She doesn't know what else to say to the child. She is the adult, and she has made her decision. It's best for River. It's best for everyone. This cabin is no longer safe.

"You will have to wear clothes. Just this one time, I need you to wear clothes. No one walks around naked. Everyone in the town wears clothes."

"Tow . . . n."

There is a sadness in this word when River says it again and celebrating it doesn't feel right anymore.

"Yes, little one. We will be traveling to town today," she says, glancing to the window, and to the wild woman somewhere beyond. "As soon as it is safe."

Adelaide doesn't know what will happen when she drops the child off with this stranger. But River's odds are better than her own. What will happen to *her*? Where will *she* go? Home, she imagines. Back to her little cabin in the woods. But who—or what—will be waiting for her?

She pushes her hand through a kitchen cabinet, looking for a meal more suitable than a snake. Behind her, River runs to the window, gazing into the forest. She practices her new word, and a few others Adelaide has not heard before.

"Tow . . . n.

Sheet.

Food.

No.

Fire.

Chic-ken.

Dead."

21

Adelaide feels protected by the kitchen window as the wild woman continues to stalk her property, but it is false protection. If the wild woman were to throw herself against the glass, it would break. If she punched or smashed a rock against the glass, it would break. Adelaide can only hope the wild woman does not discover the truth of this.

River wears the wool shirt, belted at the waist. It had not been an easy task, but Adelaide was quick, and the girl was draped and cinched before she could holler. River could've fought it, but she didn't. Perhaps the girl understands that they will be traveling today. Or perhaps she's grown tired of fighting. Adelaide accepts the victory, either way.

The wild woman, on the other hand, is problematic. Adelaide can't risk leaving for town while she is still circling the cabin, teeth bared, eyes trained on the window. But the sun will be setting soon, the journey even more strenuous in the dark.

And the men. They could be here at any moment.

She must think of something now. Now. *Goddammit, now!*

Adelaide pounds her hands against the sink, rattling dishes and startling the child.

"I'm sorry, little one. Keep eating. We'll need our strength today."

Behind her, the clock ticks away, *useless-useless-useless*. Will the mockery never cease?

She wants to grab the basket and take River's hand and run. But Adelaide needs to be patient. The wild woman has been here all day and will surely tire soon, retreat to the forest. Wherever it is that she goes. They must wait until the wild woman leaves.

But right now, the men are foremost in her mind.

If the men come for River tonight, they will likely arrive after dark, when they can make a silent and stealthy approach. Adelaide must be on the lookout for the perfect timing. After the wild woman, but before the men. It will be tricky, and Adelaide tries to dismiss her fears of everything going wrong. For all she knows, the men are surrounding her homestead right now, an angry mob armed with torches and pitchforks. *Kill the witch!*

Adelaide is focused. Ready. If she has to slash her way out of this forest, branch by branch, she will do it for the child. River deserves better. She deserves everything that Adelaide can't give her—a family, a safe home, a childhood. Catherine was right. This is no place for children.

The wild woman squats outside the garden and watches Adelaide through the window. She does not blink. A shadow blooms beneath the wild woman, and the dirt runs black as she urinates against the post, eyes locked on Adelaide. When she is finished, she does not stand. She is a gargoyle in the forest, her knees hooked, her back rigid.

Adelaide knows this game, and her fingers twitch at the blatant display of aggression. She feels for the paring knife in her pocket, with half a mind to leap through the glass and dispatch the wild woman right here, right now. Sometimes we must do savage things to protect our children. The wild woman has laid forth a challenge, but Adelaide must refrain.

For now.

The sun has lowered in the sky, but still, Adelaide must wait. There will soon come a time. But not yet.

No, not just yet.

Night has finally fallen, and the wild woman is nowhere to be seen.

Adelaide needs to extinguish all light, not only to help her eyes adjust to the night, but to prevent outsiders from peering into the cabin. She and River will need all the cover they can get. Obscurity. Safety.

Adelaide lays the heaviest firewood atop the embers in the fireplace to snuff them out, and she peers through the living room window one last time, grasping the curtains. River pulls the fabric from Adelaide's hands.

"No," the girl says.

Adelaide balks. "River! You will say no such thing to me!" She softens her voice and kneels to the girl's level. "We'll be leaving soon, little one, and it needs to be dark and quiet, so we know when it's time to go."

The girl glares at her, but ultimately relinquishes the curtain.

"Thank you," Adelaide says, as she gathers the fabric in her hands.

She pauses. Streaks mar the living room window—on the *outside* of the glass, tracing the frame. The wild woman has been testing the cabin's boundaries and is getting closer to figuring something out. Something she shouldn't. Something that makes Adelaide very nervous. Ever since Adelaide torched the farm, she'd been preparing for men. The wild woman has always been a burden, of course, but tonight, she is a threat.

And Adelaide doesn't have another plan.

She draws the heavy curtains shut, blows out the lantern, and the cabin goes black.

✿

The woman is taking the girl back to mother tonight. She can't wait to show mother the soft animal that isn't real, and her hat, the color of sweet honey.

The girl is heavy. Heavy as a stone in the water. The woman wrapped something around her, and although it is soft against her skin, the girl feels like she can't breathe, can't walk. She can't see her body anymore and wonders if it is still there. She pushes her fingers against the fabric, feels her belly, her knees, her shoulders. The girl is relieved. She is still there, even though she can't see herself. She holds out her arms, examines the fabric that is the color of a tongue. She looks more like the woman now, and less like mother.

The girl doesn't understand why they are still inside, and she turns to the woman.

"Sheet," the girl says.

But the woman is in the food room and does not respond.

That wasn't the right word. That is the word for the sleep cave. The girl tries another word. "Chic-ken."

No. Those are the round birds that don't fly.

The girl scratches her head, bangs her fingers against her eyebrow. It's a new word that she's trying to remember. The word that will make the woman bring her back to mother. It made the *oww* sound. Brother would have remembered. He's better with the woman's words than she is.

The girl shuffles closer to the food room but walking with the woman's clothes on her body is hard, and she has to kick the fabric in order to move. She stands beside the hutch.

"Town," the girl says.

The woman looks at her but turns quickly away.

"Soon," the woman says.

The girl turns this new word around in her mouth. *Sooo-nn.*

"Soooon."

"Yes," the woman says.

"Yes."

The girl is learning many new words. She likes the way *soon* sounds but doesn't know what it means. She thinks she knows what *yes* means, and this makes her happy. Yes. Town. And then she will be with mother.

The girl watches the woman in the food room. The woman who is a pretend mother. The woman looks different from the way she looked when she first took the girl and brother. Smaller. Thinner. Like she hasn't eaten for many days and many nights. There's a darkness around her eyes the color of a rain cloud. And her hurt has changed. The girl can feel it. Now, the woman's hurt is a tight, empty space, like a chest that can't breathe, like a burrow under the ground, collapsing with sand.

❧

It feels like it might be the right time. Adelaide stands at the door, counting the cracks in the wood like she hasn't memorized them a dozen times already tonight. In one fist, an overflowing basket. In the other, River's petite hand.

The disadvantage to covering the windows is that the outside is a mystery to them. Adelaide won't know who, or what, is outside her door until they emerge. But right now, all is silent, and this may be their only chance.

Adelaide wipes the sweat from her brow, and her chest rattles so furiously that she fears a sudden heart attack, just when River needs her most.

Adelaide smiles at River, who clings tightly to Little Bird's gray elephant.

So now they are ready.

Adelaide takes a moment to reassemble her bun, but yes, they are ready.

River grins at Adelaide and bounces on her heels, so she is ready.

And they *have* to be ready.

The clock behind her screams, *go-go-GO.*

Adelaide takes a deep breath, in case it is her last, and is reaching for the dead bolt when the doorknob moves. Her hand freezes in midair as someone tests it from outside her cabin.

Men. Beasts.

One and the same.

"Get away from the window," Adelaide whispers to River as the girl yanks the curtain aside, eager, expectant. Adelaide lunges for her, but River resists, pulling her wrists from Adelaide's grasp as a howl breaks the silence.

The wild woman.

River is no longer safe in these woods with the men after her. A good mother will sacrifice everything for the safety of her children. Adelaide knows this. And surely, the wild woman knows, too. If only Adelaide could speak to her, beg her to be reasonable. But Adelaide cannot speak to the wild woman, and she must do everything in her power to protect River, even from the thing she so desperately seeks.

The wild woman howls once more.

These walls have held her off before, and they will do it again.

"Please," Adelaide pleads. "Please."

Before she can utter another word, or grasp at the child once more, gravel peppers her cabin as vehicles tear into her clearing, and her home floods with brilliant white light. It pours through every window, slashing through the drapes. Chalky light, more dazzling than the sun itself, blinds Adelaide, and she stumbles backward, shielding her eyes. River throws herself against the floor and covers her head, barking syllables in her feral tongue.

Adelaide crawls to the girl, throwing her body upon her as a shield. Beneath her, River trembles.

There is no sound from outside. No more howling, no noise of any kind. There is only the light. Adelaide forces open her eyes.

"Stay down," she tells River.

Though Adelaide knows the child does not understand her words, she obeys, and Adelaide crawls to the window, keeping her head low to the ground.

Shielding her eyes with her hand, she peers through the fissures between her fingers. There are trucks on her property—two that she can see, perhaps more that she can't. Hunting lights mounted to their hoods throw beams of light against her home.

The men.

They are here.

The howling she heard earlier had not been a threat—it had been a warning.

Adelaide anticipates footsteps, hollering, breaking windows, but there is none of this—only silence. And the light.

She returns to River, circling her arms around the girl, and pulling the child around the back of the sofa.

Adelaide checks for the paring knife in her apron and then reaches for the large knife on the side table, tucking it against her thigh.

So this is the night they rip River from her arms. Let 'em try, she thinks, gripping the knife tighter. Let 'em try.

But there is no pounding on Adelaide's door. No barking dogs. No threatening words from enraged men. Only silence. Minutes go by like this, maybe hours.

When the lights finally abate, Adelaide and River are left in a blackness so complete that Adelaide can't see her fingers inches from her face, and she blinks against a darkness that is more harrowing than the light itself. She locates the side table, replacing the knife, and then lifts a trembling River from the floor.

With the girl tucked safely in her arms, Adelaide peers through her living room window. The lights may be gone, but the trucks remain. Adelaide feels a path through the dark cabin, laying River into a nest of blankets on her bed, nearly falling atop the girl.

River is motionless, her eyes vacant. Adelaide shakes her.

"River," she says. "Come back to me, little one."

Nothing.

"We have to leave now, and I can't carry you. Town, remember?"

A blink, and a tilt of the head.

"There we are. Sit up. Good girl."

Adelaide rushes to the living room and grabs the basket, slipping the large knife inside, before returning to River.

"I wanted this to be easier," she says as she unbolts the latch and pushes open the bedroom window. She lifts River and helps her through the gap, one leg at a time, and then drops the basket to the earth beside the girl.

Adelaide has one foot on the ground and one foot still inside the cabin when she smells the smoke. It is unmistakable.

Something is burning.

Adelaide hopes it is only a figment of her imagination. But there, beyond her bedroom window, near the back of her property—fire.

The chicken coop.

No.

Black smoke smolders into the air, the flames a russet glow.

Adelaide slips into the night to stand beside River against the cabin. The window slams shut behind her, and she knows the men have heard it, but she can't bring herself to leave the shelter of her home just yet.

River squeals, and points to the garden, which is now aflame as well.

Adelaide can do nothing but stand beneath the eave of her cabin and watch it burn. The moist air has already begun to choke the outermost flames, but the center of the fire is a boiling crimson. Smoke billows upward, breaking through the forest canopy.

Somewhere in the distance, Henry's gravelly cry shears the night in two.

22

The breeze slams against Adelaide's shoulder as she watches the fire in her garden soar toward the canopy. River pulls away, but Adelaide holds firm to the girl's hand.

Adelaide cannot breathe. The wattle fence, the garden beds, the mulch, the vines and the weeds she pulled from the grave—and Little Bird, oh god, Little Bird—all ablaze, fire licking the night sky, the heat evaporating the tears as they fall down her cheeks.

Henry emerges from the shadows and stumbles toward the cabin.

Zelda is not with him, and Adelaide cannot bring herself to look back at the burning coop.

Henry stands beside Adelaide in mourning. His feathers, usually white and plum, are now gray and charred, lying in clumps across his already ragged body. She squats beside her beloved bird, her calves screaming, and brushes ash from his feathers, smoothing them across his back.

"Oh, Henry. What will become of us now?"

He chortles, despite his heartache.

Adelaide wants to comfort the bird, but they can wait no longer.

She pulls River away from the cabin and sneaks into the clearing at the back of her property. The child stumbles, cries out, but Adelaide does not turn back. She is scared they've waited too long already, and they'll be attacked halfway down the road to town, lights in the distance offering freedom, but not for them. Not for a frightened old lady and an uncivilized child who didn't leave soon enough, didn't run fast enough.

Adelaide glances behind her. There are no men on their heels. But that could all change in the time it takes her to swallow the lump in her throat.

Adelaide and River move quickly. Away from the cabin, past the burning chicken coop, through a small clearing and toward a cluster of trees near the mountain road.

She yanks on River's arm to pull her closer, and together, they bound over roots and disappear into the shadows.

Adelaide can almost see the road now.

Yes, there it is. Just ahead.

They are almost there. Almost free.

A roar echoes all around them, and Adelaide freezes in her steps, River crashing into the back of her legs.

The wild woman roars again, no breath in between, and Adelaide tries to cover her ears. The sound—like an infant, like a tornado—surrounds them, so deafening that even little River flinches and closes her eyes.

Adelaide doesn't know where to look. The wild woman could be anywhere.

Adelaide curses the moonless sky. Blackness is all around her, but the wild woman must be able to see her because the sound begins to circle them.

When Adelaide looks up, the gravel road is farther away than ever before.

River pulls from Adelaide's grip, but the old woman holds firm.

"No!" she whispers. Or maybe she screamed. Adelaide cannot tell in the silence that follows. River twists her fingers, and Adelaide fights to hang on to the child. Her daughter.

"Please, no."

The wild woman, merely a shadow, darts past Adelaide so fast that the air rushes around her. She drops the basket and it tumbles away. Adelaide clutches River's hand with both of her own. The air is bitterly cold, but even in this chill, River's fingers sweat and slip, digit by digit, from Adelaide's grip. She squeezes until her knuckles pop, until her fingertips throb with pressure. But the child is strong and determined, and with a whoop and a grunt, River pulls free.

Adelaide collapses to the ground in the near-perfect darkness, breathless, listening to two little feet disappear into the forest.

23

River vanished so quickly. Adelaide listened for as long as she could, but as the girl ran farther, the sound of her footsteps dissipated like a dream in the morning.

Adelaide spins her head from side to side, looking for River, her cabin, or even the gravel road so she can orient herself, but every direction is exactly the same. There is nothing but darkness, as if she has lost her sight completely. She swings her arms all around her but finds nothing, hears nothing.

Adelaide drops to her knees and inches forward, fumbling over boxes of food and other basket debris she cannot see.

Behind her, another roar. If she didn't know better, Adelaide would swear there is a mountain lion in her woods this night.

Her breath tides in and out of her throat, deep, dry swallows that satisfy nothing.

The sound of the wild woman tunneling through the trees is replaced by the sound of approaching trucks. The darkness is replaced by brilliant white light.

This night is not yet over.

The men have found her.

❀

The girl stands with mother and looks to the woman one last time.

Even though she is with mother now, part of the girl wants to stay with the woman. The girl does not understand why she feels this way, because the woman is not a mother. But lately, the girl's heart can barely tell the difference. She holds the woman's shirt tightly around her body and smells the fabric. It smells like the woman, and everything in the woman's home all at once. It smells like the food room, and the fireplace, and the sofa, and the round birds that don't fly, and the woman's own breath and skin.

The girl hears a loud sound and looks up. In the clearing, there are big shapes and big light—light brighter than the morning.

The girl wants to help the woman, but mother holds her tight, leading her backward, into the brush.

The girl cannot take her eyes off the woman in the middle of all the light. She is like the fire inside the cabin. A piece of tree glowing like the sun.

❀

River is gone, and there is nothing left for the men to take.

Adelaide shields her eyes against the barrage and faces the two men before her. The brothers stand side by side, hands on their hips, leaning away from each other as though ricocheting from the same point in opposite directions.

Adelaide squints through the headlights, seeking the old man. She knows he is here; she can feel him.

Goddamn it, show yourself.

She detects a third car—an old sedan parked on the road, no lights; a black hole in the otherwise brilliant clearing.

There he is.

From the back of one of the trucks comes the sound of furious scratching, shaking metal. A cage of hounds.

"There's nothing for you here," Adelaide chokes out, spittle falling from her lips. "Not anymore."

The brothers do not respond. She can feel their rage, their fear.

She reminds herself that these men—these boys—are merely following orders. They are not the ones in charge.

Adelaide speaks again. "I'm alone. The child is gone."

The figures look to each other, an odd spinning of the heads.

"What'd you say, witch?"

It's impossible for her to tell which man spoke.

"There is no one else here. You're wasting your time."

"We'll see 'bout that. And don't go thinkin' we're stupid. We know there's two."

Adelaide grasps her abdomen as though punched. Her Little Bird, in the garden. On fire, yet safe from these men, nonetheless.

"Get off my property," she says, her words less forceful than she had intended.

This is a battle she cannot win, and there is nothing left to fight for. Not anymore. Adelaide puts her hands in the air, a surrender.

"Look," she begins.

One of the young men lunges forward, plowing into Adelaide's shoulder. If she were a younger woman, she could've taken the blow, perhaps dealt one of her own. But she is an old woman now, and she did not have time to brace her tired bones against it. Adelaide spins through the air, colliding with the ground. All she can see is white and black, and a few sparkling stars that trail through her vision.

A growl emanates from the brush. Not a woman's growl, but a child's growl, high in pitch and edged with panic.

The man turns to his brother, smiles. "And there we are."

Adelaide gasps for air. She claws at the ground, bits of rock ripping her fingernails, as she hauls her body from the dirt.

"Get away!" she screams into the forest, at the men, at River.

Adelaide pulls herself to her knees, her head spinning. She stands and looks for the brothers, finally spotting them within the thicket that borders her driveway. Trees block the light from the trucks, and even this close, Adelaide can barely see the men.

One of the brothers squats to the ground, hand held out as though luring a feral cat. His voice is high and lilting, but Adelaide can't make out his words.

The lights illuminate the basket and Adelaide rushes to it, fetching the large knife tucked within. She stumbles toward the men, toward the shadows, thrusting the blade forward, left and right, everywhere.

"Leave her alone," she pleads.

But Adelaide's words are like smoke, evaporating into the air, ignored. She steps closer, peering into darkness.

She soon spots River, leaning forward on all fours, teeth bared, growling. She is a nocturnal animal—no longer Adelaide's daughter, nor the little girl holding a stuffed gray elephant in front of the fire.

River lunges forward but is pulled back into shadow as the wild woman clutches her daughter. But River is determined, and she struggles against her mother, barking threats at the men. The wild woman tries to stay hidden, while River strives to be seen, heard, feared.

A figure emerges from the old sedan. Thinner than the boys, frailer. But as strong as he ever was.

The old man is a black silhouette against the beams. He leans against his car and lights a cigarette, bringing it to his mouth. Watching. Waiting. He shields his eyes, struggling to see across the clearing and into the trees.

River spits. Hollers. She ticks and screeches—all the sounds of her feral tongue at once. She throws her weight forward, pulling against the resistance of her mother.

Adelaide cannot allow River to put herself at risk, and she shrieks into the night, rushing toward the men.

Her feet stumble over stones, and she falls, unable to keep her footing. She swings the knife in her hand, but it lands on nothing, spinning from her grasp and into the trees as she crashes atop them, biting, scratching, kicking.

The element of surprise has given her an edge. She has won this small battle.

And then she has lost.

Suddenly, Adelaide is on her back, the night sky spinning above her, a fist landing in her gut.

❋

Mother lifts the girl and carries her through the trees.

The girl fights mother, and kicks mother, and pushes her body against mother, and they fall to the ground like the woman fell to the ground.

She can't leave the woman by herself with all the hurt. But mother says, No. Mother says, We must run.

The girl breaks free of mother's arms, heading back to the clearing, but mother is quickly behind her, grabbing her, and they are on the ground again, under a sky with no moon.

Mother holds her so tightly.

Mother doesn't know the woman who sleep-breathes loudly, and who makes sweet things to eat, and who taught her and brother to say new words like, *fire* and *chicken* and *sheet*. Or who gave her a special name that no one else knows.

The girl tells mother everything at once. She tells her about the fat flowers that are the color of the sun, growing upside down in the woman's window. She tells mother about the small river that comes out of a shiny thing in the food room. And that the woman can make water whenever she wants, and make daylight whenever she wants, like a piece of sun in a jar.

She tells mother how the woman kept her safe. And that they stayed up all night in the snow trying to save brother.

That she held them, like a mother. And loved them, like a mother.

Mother looks surprised when the girl says this, but she listens as the girl cries.

Then she does not need our help, mother says, because she is very strong.

And the girl says, Yes, but not as strong as you.

The girl pushes herself up, but mother holds her back. She growls at mother—just for a moment—and mother's eyes get big, and they get mad, but the girl doesn't care. She has to take the woman's hurt away so she can stop hurting, too. Mother pulls her to the ground and stands above her. She puts a hand to the girl's chest, and when the girl hears mother's words, she can breathe again because mother is going to make everything better.

Mother says, Stay quiet, stay small, stay hidden. I'll be back for you.

The girl watches mother bound through the forest, by hand and by foot, back toward the clearing. Back toward the woman with all the hurt.

✿

24

A figure leaps from the trees, and the brothers fall away from Adelaide.

She retches into the dirt and pushes onto her elbows. The brothers landed a few punches to her ribs, a few kicks to her side before everything began to spin. Adelaide touches her face. Her teeth are intact. Her eyes are not swollen, and her nose is not broken. They've spared her that.

Adelaide hears screams from deep in the thicket. A man.

She hauls herself to her knees and looks around for River as the other man—Brother #1—dashes back toward the trucks and the blinding light.

Another scream.

There is no going back—this ends tonight.

Adelaide stands and follows the sound into the darkness.

Just ahead, a dark puddle stains the earth. And there, beyond the densest tree cluster, she spots them.

The wild woman clings to Brother #2, her arms wrapped around the man's neck, her elbows folding in on his throat. She is bloody, and he is bloody, the battle vicious but equal.

Brother #2 fights her, but is no match for an angry mother, and he collapses from her grasp, clawing at his shattered windpipe.

A car door slams, and Adelaide turns, watching Brother #1 rush back to the thicket, his footsteps growing louder, closer. And he has something in his hands.

Two sharp noises clack across the clearing as he racks the shotgun.

The wild woman straightens to her full height, standing above the gasping man on the ground. Clawing for air. Begging for air. His jaw practically dislocates as he tries to scream, managing only a whistle, a gurgle.

And then Brother #2 is motionless in the dirt.

A shotgun blast rings through the night, and Adelaide clutches her head, the sound like a bolt of lightning to her skull.

"Hey!" Brother #1 calls out, as if such a simple word can stop everything. As if such a simple word can undo it all.

The hounds snarl and scream into the night, slamming against the metal crate in the truck, desperate for release.

Brother #1 lifts the shotgun to his shoulder and locks his legs. He becomes a hunter, still and calm.

The wild woman growls, spittle foaming at her lips. She is preparing to leap toward Brother #1 when he releases two clacks of sound and fires into the clearing.

The wild woman screams—a horror of a scream, an anomaly of a scream—and she whirls into the shadows.

✿

Mother falls into the dirt and the pale rain and the girl runs to her. Mother is hurt and her blood is on the girl's hands. It is the color of the bird that makes the *yeep* sound.

The girl asks, Are you very hurt?

Mother says, No. Only a little hurt.

Little hurt is better than big hurt.

As the girl watches mother struggle to stand, she knows they should run away, but she can still feel the woman in the clearing. The woman is in danger, and the girl wants to help. She *needs* to help. Because the woman is kind. But she is not strong like mother.

The girl shakes out of the soft thing the woman wrapped around her so she can run better, and mother says, No.

Her heart pounds in her chest like thunder when it rains.

Mother stands and screams, NO!, but the girl is already running through the trees, mother reaching and spinning behind her.

❦

The wild woman was nothing more than a fading shadow to Adelaide, an animal returning to the forest.

Brother #1 racks the shotgun once more. Two clacks of sound. He trains the gun on the trees, but the wild woman has vanished.

He slings the shotgun over his shoulder and falls to the ground beside his lifeless brother.

"Daddy!" he yells from the shadows.

The young man pounds his brother's chest. He screams, his voice like an ice pick to Adelaide's skull. He punches the dirt, punches the rocks, rips the shotgun from his shoulder and slams it against the base of a tree, over and over again, raining bark all around.

"Daddy!"

Adelaide tucks farther into the darkness and peers around the thicket. The trees have taken a beating, dozens of small holes marring their mighty trunks. Buckshot.

A spray of blood streaks the clearing, and Adelaide hopes that the wild woman will once again survive the cruelties of them all.

River emerges from the blackness, crouching on all fours. She is nude, having shed the shirt Adelaide wrapped around her only hours before. River advances toward Brother #1, and Adelaide reaches for the girl.

No.

River bares her teeth. Her eyes are wild, crazed, the sight of them sending a shiver up Adelaide's spine.

No.

Brother #1 sees her, too. His face is scarlet, sheeting with sweat. River doesn't cower and she doesn't advance. Her eyes are locked on the man. Behind her, the wild woman stumbles forward, struggling to stand. Howling for her daughter.

Adelaide lunges toward Brother #1, and he turns, his arm whipping across his chest, spinning her backward through the air. Adelaide trembles against the cold ground, cradling her head, testing her jaw.

And then River leaps from the shadows.

The child wraps her body around Brother #1's neck, but she is small—*so small*—and her arms and legs barely grasp his torso. The man stumbles back, the shotgun falling from his shoulders, clattering against stone.

River will not win. She is not big enough, not strong enough. A fierce little beast, but a child all the same.

The wild woman screams. She, too, knows the truth.

Adelaide throws herself atop the shotgun, pulling it into her lap. She aims it at the man. But River is there, and Adelaide cannot risk it.

She aims at his legs, wondering if that will be enough distance for buckshot. Will she hurt River? She hopes not, pleads not. She has no choice.

But then Brother #1 falls to his knees, and as River tumbles across the ground, Adelaide snatches her finger from the trigger.

The girl is fast, uninjured, and she launches at the man once again.

"What the hell's goin' on over there?" The old man's voice echoes from across the clearing above the cacophony of his kenneled hounds.

She'll never save the girl now.

Brother #1 spins wildly through the trees, ripping River's legs from his chest, punching at her small arms enveloping his neck.

But River does not cry out with pain. She does not flinch.

She meets Adelaide's gaze for only a moment before sinking her teeth into Brother #1's neck.

The girl stays latched to his throat as his voice turns to mud, as his arms fall from her torso, as his knees slide out from beneath him.

Dogs bark, tumbling from their crate, hungry for excitement, the old man in pursuit.

Adelaide bolts toward River, and the pain in her abdomen flares. She'll never be able to handle the weight of both the weapon and the girl, so Adelaide drops the shotgun and launches herself at River, throwing the child over her shoulder.

River barks mutilated sounds and stunted syllables into the trees, blood sheeting from her jaw like an oil slick.

Adelaide runs toward her cabin as the old man races with his hounds to the thicket. To Brother #1 and Brother #2. His sons. He doesn't yet know what has happened here this night. But he will soon.

The hounds spill as a single wave through the clearing, but when they spot Adelaide and River, they change course, their paws tangling in the glare of the headlights, as they surge anew toward the cabin.

But Adelaide is there first and she throws open the door, hurling River into the cabin.

The dogs draw closer. Teeth bared, like River. Growling, like River.

We are not getting out of this alive.

This is the thought that lodges in Adelaide's mind as she throws her weight into the cabin, pulling the door closed behind her just in time.

25

For a moment, everything is as it should be. Nothing rattles or falls from the shelves. The curtains billow as the breeze subsides. The lantern sits on the side table, right where she left it. The fireplace still blazes, even though Adelaide attempted to snuff it out before they left the cabin.

Adelaide would almost feel safe, if not for the dogs throwing themselves against her door.

Their collective weight thunders against the wood, and Adelaide wrangles the bolt into the locked position. She can only hope it holds. Behind her, somehow louder than the dogs, her clock ticks like a prophecy, *dead-dead-dead.*

Adelaide feels for the paring knife in her apron pocket, relieved to find it still in place.

The truck lights beam through her bedroom windows, and Adelaide finds River hiding above the kitchen hutch, where she first discovered the dirty bodies of two feral children in her home. The girl has folded herself tightly into the corner, the lower half of her face streaked with drying blood, her eyes large and pallid. That bewitchment they once held now gone, replaced by something that should never exist in the gaze of a child.

Adelaide reaches out to the girl, and River tumbles into her outstretched arms, hands grasping at her back. The girl smells of blood and soil, but Adelaide clings tightly, breathing in her scent as best she can.

She wishes there was somewhere to run, somewhere to hide. There are dark corners, cupboards, a small closet in her bedroom, but none of these places will conceal them forever.

"I'm so sorry, little one," she says to River as she collapses with the child onto the sofa.

The dogs bay outside her door. Their nails tear at the wood.

A knock.

Adelaide cups the girl's face, and River leans her forehead against Adelaide's.

A second knock, slow and drawn out.

In the distance, a sorrowful howl. The wild woman seeks her daughter still.

At the door, wood splinters beneath determined claws. And then the old man's voice, "Enough," and the dogs go quiet.

Something explodes against the door, metal clanging against metal. Twice now. Three times. Another.

Adelaide grabs the girl by the shoulders and shoves her toward the kitchen.

"Hide!"

River stumbles against the sink as the front door explodes, and Adelaide cries out, collapsing onto the sofa. Beneath her, the chain under the floorboard rattles.

The old man stands in the doorway, flanked by dogs who now sprawl at their master's feet. In his eyes is that same dark shimmer that Adelaide has tried to forget all her life.

In his hand is the shotgun.

He enters her home.

Adelaide had meant to stand tall against him, show him ferocity. Strength. But he is here. Again. And Adelaide tucks farther into her sofa, unable to look him in the eyes.

Instead, she looks to his cheeks, his forehead, his chin—anything to avoid those eyes. Adelaide studies every pore, every wrinkle. His skin is like a full moon, craters edged by the flickering light of the fire. He has changed so much, yet he is the same man.

And she is the same woman.

He peers around her living room as if he's never seen it before. It is the same, if only a bit paler, disfigured by time.

As they both are.

Please. Please, don't look in the kitchen.

Adelaide hears no sound from River, and hopes she is hidden. Once again on top of the hutch, perhaps. Or tucked into a cabinet. Before she can control herself, Adelaide turns her head.

River is there. She stands limp at the sink, eyes wide, mouth slack.

Adelaide is horrified. The girl is so conspicuous standing in the middle of the room. River does not growl. She does not crouch, readying for an attack. Her fury has gone silent.

The old man is different from the rest—Adelaide has always known this. The air is tight and heavy, buzzing with a strange energy. Something dangerous and uncertain. And now River feels it, too.

The man lingers in the doorway. He lights a cigarette and gazes intently at his fingers, as though reading prophecy in the smoke.

He wears no coat and does not seem to be shivering despite the chill pouring into the cabin. His cigarette leaves ruby trails in the air as he inhales only once, before snuffing it out on her wall. A small nugget of fire rolls from the wood and smolders on her floor. Adelaide wills it to ignite at his feet and consume him in flame, but the old man grinds it into dust with his boot, leaving a black scar in the wood.

It's all Adelaide can stare at—that little black mark. A black mark, next to her broken door, in a cabin surrounded by a dead son, a burnt garden, and in her kitchen, a bloodstained little girl.

He walks toward her, but she cannot take her eyes from the burn mark on her floor. He is so close that she can smell him now, his scent of sweat.

From the corner of her eye, a flash of light—the fireplace glinting off the barrel of the shotgun slung over his shoulder. She can still feel the weight of it in her own hands, and she curses herself for leaving it behind. Maybe she could have carried both the gun and the child. They might have made it to the cabin before the dogs caught up to them. It's possible; she should have tried.

She can't bear the silence. It is louder than the shattering of her door. Louder than the screaming in her head. Louder even than the clock behind her, still regurgitating, *dead-dead-dead*.

The sofa sinks as the old man sits beside her, and Adelaide braids her fingers against her stomach and holds her breath.

Everything in the cabin swirls around her, his proximity like a splinter lodged in her heart.

At least he has not seen River.

The old man slips the shotgun from his shoulder, leaning the weapon against the sofa.

(His arms. His hands. Squeezing. Pushing. That's what she feels.)

He exhales into his palms, and his breath fills the small room.

(His stench on her body, thrust from the recesses of his lungs. That's what Adelaide smells.)

He cradles his head in his hands, falling over his knees.

(His arched back, pulsing, sweating. It's all she sees.)

With the old man beside her, Adelaide is twenty years old again. Self-sufficient, but lonely. That knock on her door. Checking her hair in a full-length mirror that once hung in her bedroom—the mirror that would reveal to her, only a few short months later, a new future, like a witch's magic mirror—before approaching the door. That knocking. So persistent. She hears it again. She is there again. Her petite hand reaching for the doorknob. Could she have stopped it? Likely not. But maybe. Expecting a camper, a lost hiker. Maybe a distant neighbor or a friend from town. Opened the door with a smile is what she did, way back then, when she was a young woman. Those dark, bewitching eyes. A beautiful stranger. Handsome, older. Skin deeply tanned. He'd smiled.

She had sensed something about him, even back then, before she knew. When he smiled, she lost her own. The air changed. The energy changed. Despite his alluring eyes, his boyish grin, she wanted to close the door, deny his request for water.

But she was young. *Stupid.* And so innocent. *Fool.* And she didn't want to be rude.

The reality of it all is jarring. Things could have been different, if only she hadn't opened the door. Perhaps. But now here she sits. And here he sits.

Before Adelaide can settle on a sentence or an action to take, the old man begins to cry. His sobs are deep, trapped in his chest, and he struggles to hold them back as they burst into his palms. Adelaide can see fragments of his face through the gaps of his fingers. He grimaces into his hands, teeth bared. His back convulses, and Adelaide resists the urge to place her hand on his shoulders. It is an automatic response to such emotion, and she chastises herself for forgetting where she is, Who he is.

Somehow the old man's grief is more frightening to her than his anger. Adelaide knows anger. She can anticipate the actions that follow anger. But his sorrow elicits compassion from Adelaide, and the conflict is bewildering.

She grips the armrest of the sofa, pulling herself as far away from the old man as she can manage, and she looks into the kitchen.

River is still there, but just barely. She has tucked herself into a dark corner, and only her frightened eyes and the curve of her legs are visible.

Good, Adelaide thinks.

Adelaide stares at the burn mark on her floor while she waits for whatever comes next. The spot sways and swells in her vision, and she wills it to grow large enough to swallow her and River whole.

❀

The woman is hurt. More hurt than before. The girl feels it all the way down into her toes, but she feels it in her heart most of all. Like her chest is going to fall off her body and sink through the ground, leaving only her arms and legs and head behind. The girl doesn't understand how the woman can walk around with this much hurt. It's like she is very sick, and the girl doesn't understand how the woman doesn't die from it.

The man looks a little bit like the woman, but he feels very different. He hurts, too, but it is not the same kind of hurt. The man's hurt is like a worm living in his belly. Like the small, fat worms that the girl, brother, and mother used to eat—the ones that live underneath the skin of a tree. The ones that pinch your lips, taking little chunks of your flesh before you bite down and eat them. That's what his hurt is like. And the girl doesn't know how to help a hurt like that, so she tries her best not to feel it.

The girl looks to the top of the hutch, where she hid with brother before they learned that the woman was kind and not scary. It is dark up there. It could hide her again. The girl wants to curl up in those shadows, way up high, and go to sleep. And when she wakes up, maybe it will be a long time ago, before mother was ever hurt in the square forest, and before brother went away forever.

She tastes blood in her mouth—blood from the man outside who hurt mother and the woman.

The woman turns and looks at the girl, and the girl knows she is going to have to do it again. She is going to have to make this man go away forever. She hopes she is strong enough.

The woman is not a mother, not really. If she were really a mother, she would bite the man's throat right now. She would know that he is rotten like the fruit mother tells her not to eat from the ground once the flies come, and she would run away. The woman doesn't understand, but the girl does.

Somewhere outside, mother runs and calls for the girl.

A dog whines in the doorway.

The girl decides that she will not hide on top of the hutch, in the dark shadows. She needs to help the woman. And teach the woman how to be brave.

The girl inches away from the corner, just a little. She waits for the right time. And when that time comes, she will help the woman get away from the man with the worms under his skin.

❧

Adelaide roots through her mind, looking for anything that might bring her strength. She hates herself. She's a goddamned coward.

Finally, the old man speaks.

"My boys," he says, his voice trailing away.

Adelaide turns from him, staring at her own reflection distorted in the glass globe of her lantern. She claws at the side of the sofa, her distress leaving tunnels through the fraying fabric.

"Those were my boys," he states plainly, "and now they're gone."

Outside the doorway, his hounds watch. They are on alert, awaiting a signal from their master, awaiting the permission to do something, *anything*.

Adelaide sits between the dogs and the old man, contemplating which she fears more, as she slips a hand into her apron and withdraws the paring knife.

River emerges from the shadows.

No.

The dried blood on her face paints her like a warrior. But warrior or not, this man is different from the others, and River is just a little girl. Adelaide widens her eyes and shakes her head, trying to hide the motion.

The hounds watch from the door. Their eyes are large and hopeful, their ears high and jostling in the breeze, as if they want to play. But Adelaide knows that all it takes is one command, one flick of the wrist from the old man.

The girl can be fast. So Adelaide will need to be faster. She *has* to be faster. Adelaide wraps her fingers around the thin hilt of the knife.

Her blade stands no chance against a gun, but the shotgun leans against the sofa, forgotten. For the moment.

The old man continues to stare forward, nodding to himself, speaking to himself. "They were all I had."

For a brief moment, Adelaide feels pity for the man. She knows what it's like to be in over your head. To regret. To lose a child. Her first child, in a way. And now another, buried in her garden. She's likely the only person for miles who knows how he feels.

Part of Adelaide thinks that if she waits long enough, stays quiet long enough, the old man will leave. He's lost so much already. Perhaps more blood need not be shed this night. Perhaps he will leave as suddenly as he arrived. She would have considered this, would have trusted in this hope—were it not for River. The girl is almost to the sofa now, and Adelaide can no longer expect the man to make a quiet exit.

It has to be now.

Adelaide swallows the lump in her throat and twists her body so that she might have a chance at him. Should she aim for his chest? His neck? His eye? Adelaide doesn't want a struggle. She doesn't want to have to do it twice. Once. *Just once.*

The old man glides his hand toward her thigh, but she is rigid, unable to pull away.

The blade trembles in her grip, but he does not see it. Or he does not care.

When the weight of his hand presses into her flesh, Adelaide gasps.

His touch is warm, yet she shivers beneath it. She is young again. He is imposing again. And strong. *Very strong.* So much power he has over her in that one small touch.

But she has the knife. She has it! It's in her hand, *goddammit!*

Adelaide opens her mouth to speak, but nothing comes out. She wants his hand gone. She wants it off her skin, but she can't think. *Can't think.*

And she can't tear her eyes from his. They have her. And they are changing. His mouth settles into a large fissure across his face.

"You know," he begins, (Adelaide wants to scream; *he is touching her leg and speaking to her, and he is mere inches from her face,* and she wants to scream.) "the polite thing to do is offer me a glass of water."

26

Adelaide is gone. She ceases to exist, here on her sofa.

A gust of wind surges through the broken door, blazing the fire anew. A log pops, and Adelaide jumps. The old man tightens his grip on her thigh.

Sometimes there is little difference between beasts and men.

"Shhh," he comforts. "It's only the wind."

Adelaide clenches the knife in her fist.

"Never mind 'bout the water," he says. "I know you and me got history. And I don't expect any kindness."

The old man looks to his hounds growing more and more restless on the steps. He lowers a hand through the air, and they struggle to calm down. One dog refuses, prancing on his front paws, whining.

"I didn't want this to happen," he utters through a clenched jaw. "I only came for my children."

The man removes his hand from Adelaide's leg and wipes his nose with a cloth from his back pocket. He replaces the cloth. He replaces his hand.

"But I'll tell you somethin' you already know," he says, his voice hoarse. "They're more mine than they are yours."

He sighs deeply.

"And I'll tell you somethin' else you already know."

River creeps closer to the sofa.

"You won't win this."

Adelaide's eyes water. She swallows back what feels like an anvil. The knife trembles in her hand.

The old man continues. "I never wanted to come back here, you know. I was happy enough to leave you be." He spreads his hands. "Yet here I am. And I've lost my boys. Because of you."

His voice is louder now. Sharper. River emerges from below the armrest of the sofa.

"I'm sittin' here tryin' to decide somethin'," he says.

River's nose. Her cheeks. Her shoulders.

"Do I take what I came for?"

Her hands. Her knees.

"Or does somethin' need to be done?"

A bark from the doorway.

The old man points through the door, outside the cabin, his finger crooked and trembling. "Does somethin' need to be done *about that?*"

Adelaide sees something in the old man's face she hadn't noticed before. Frailty. His cheekbones—high and sharp. His eyes—still dark and bewitching, but whites stained yellow with time, a thick burst of red at the corners. An abyss below them—cavernous, paper skin, spiderweb veins.

But old man or not, Adelaide knows he will kill them both tonight.

She tries to remind herself that, in the end, it doesn't matter. There are no magnificent deaths. She has done all she can for herself, and for River. She can do no more. She is no mother bear. Perhaps she never was.

And then the old man sees River as she inches closer, her skin straining over rigid muscle.

The old man leans forward. His gaze softens, and he smiles. The dogs stand alert, watching River. Watching everything.

River growls and they become uneasy, spinning in place, barking, ears twitching.

Beside Adelaide, the old man speaks.

"Well, aren't you even prettier than—"

Adelaide moves before she has time to reconsider, and the old man falls silent. Maybe he forgot what he was going to say. Or maybe he saw the knife flashing in the light—the knife Adelaide now holds, arcing toward him.

The blade sinks into the old man's hand, through skin and muscle, and comes out the other side, lodging into Adelaide's thigh.

The old man roars, and snatches his hand from her leg, splitting Adelaide's skin. She cries out, buckling to the floor.

The dogs erupt. Yelping. Salivating. But River snarls, and they do not enter.

The old man stands and rises above her. He cradles his hand, blood seeping down his pants and onto the floor, his face like a bomb ready to detonate.

❀

The dogs are so loud that the girl cannot think. One enters the cabin and the girl doesn't know what to do to make him go away. Her mind is full of holes, like the tunnels through the trees that those small, fat worms leave behind. Yes, that's what her mind is like.

The girl growls.

It is a growl like the kind mother makes—soft and deep, because loud is not always scarier.

The sound travels down, past the girl's throat, where it goes into her chest and then her belly, before coming back up and out of her mouth. The dogs are scared of her, and so she growls at the dogs again and makes them even more scared.

One of the dogs leaps forward, looking into the girl's big eyes.

The girl looks into the dog's big eyes, and he takes a step back.

The others stay behind the first, but they watch, and the girl growls at them, too, and they cry. They are not brave, so they do not enter the cabin.

The woman crawls toward her, leaving her blood in a line across the floor. The girl can smell it. She thinks the dogs can smell it, too, and the girl tells them, No. Go away. She says these things the same way she would have said them to brother if he were here, and she needed to say no, or go away. But the dogs do not know her words. Sometimes you don't need to understand the same words to make someone feel something, and the girl growls again—deeper, scarier—and the dogs back away from the door.

The woman reaches for the girl, says words to her, but the girl does not hear them. The girl is watching the man coming closer to them, growing taller, and the girl wants *his* blood to leave a line on the floor.

She growls at the dogs once more and then leaps at the old man. She can already taste his blood in her mouth.

❁

Adelaide screams as River launches over her. She reaches for the girl, but is too slow, her reflexes further muddied by pain.

The hounds bay at the door. They leap and circle the steps, staring at Adelaide with predator eyes, ready to bite, destroy. She doesn't understand why they have not entered.

The old man hurls himself across the living room, launching River from his back. She lands on the sofa, legs spinning above her like an overturned crab. She barks angry syllables, and pulls herself upright, leaping at the man once more.

Behind her, the dogs test the boundaries of the cabin. Stepping in. Stepping out. Howling.

The old man screams as River sinks her teeth into his arm.

Adelaide can see the knife still lodged through his hand, the handle protruding from between the bones. She can get to it. She must.

Adelaide pulls herself to her knees, gripping the side table for support, but it collapses beneath her weight, and the lantern explodes against the ground. Adelaide careens backward, slipping on the lantern fluid now dripping down her skirt and pooling among shards of broken glass.

The girl tries to bite the old man's neck, but she cannot reach.

She kicks at his body, but she is too small.

The old man reels backward, grunting as he thrusts the child over his shoulder, launching River across the room. She slams against the wall, and the knife spins from the old man's hand, clattering to the ground.

Adelaide scrambles toward it. She no longer feels the pain in her chest, the gash across her leg, or the puddle of cold lantern fluid sheeting down her legs. There is only the knife in her hand.

Adelaide stands. Behind her, the clock ticks, finally offering solidarity.

Yes-yes-yes.

She holds the blade out before her. Ready.

Ready.

Adelaide rises. She can barely see the old man in the corner of her living room, but she can see the barrel of his shotgun, the muzzle—clogged with dirt and marred by rock—mere inches from her face.

The blade in her hand is suddenly absurd, but she tightens her grip anyway.

"Why do you make everything so *goddamned difficult?*"

His voice echoes across the small room, and Adelaide nearly crumples to the floor.

"I should kill you right now. Both of you."

Adelaide closes her eyes.

"Goddamn it."

Adelaide waits.

"I came for one thing. One goddamned thing."

She waits to die.

"I lost my boys 'cause of you."

Silence fills the room, and Adelaide braves a peek at the old man.

He shudders before her, the shotgun swaying in his grip. Adelaide takes a small step back, shifting the knife to a better position in her hand.

Behind him, River stands and stumbles, her head bobbing from side to side.

The old man grasps the thickest part of the shotgun, and Adelaide holds her breath.

"Goddamn," he says, the word erupting from his lips. He exhales in a long whistle.

"I know you didn't hurt my boys. I know it wasn't you." Though his words are lenient, his voice is harsh, enraged.

The old man adjusts the shotgun, holding it more like a stick than a weapon. He tucks his injured hand against his chest and dips his chin toward it.

"You 'n me got history, but now I came for what's mine, and I ain't leavin' empty-handed."

He points the shotgun at River.

"I'm takin' her with me, and you ain't gonna stop me," he says.

"So take her," Adelaide says, hardening her grip around the knife, and stepping closer to the beast moving toward her daughter.

❉

The room spins around the girl. Her body hurts. More than all of the woman's hurt, and mother's hurt, and the man's hurt, all bundled together. The man's fingers have left spots on her arms. The spots burn, like he is still holding her. Like he is still hurting her.

The girl stands by the fire and waits for her legs to become strong. She is not scared. Not anymore.

Maybe a little scared.

The girl is so close to the fire that she can feel it on her skin. She touched it once, many moons ago. She can still feel the hurt if she rubs her fingers together.

The man is stronger than the girl. And braver than the girl. But the girl stands by the fire. And she knows that fire hurts.

The girl reaches into the fireplace, clenching her teeth against the hurt on her skin, the smell of her burning hair. She stands before the man, brave as mother, holding her weapon—a piece of tree glowing like the sun.

❉

27

Adelaide dodges the log as it soars across the room, fire sailing past the old man's head.

It lands with a clatter at her front door, smoldering and flickering. The dogs scamper away from the opening to yap at her cabin from afar, their bodies retreating into the night.

River reaches into the fireplace for another piece of burning wood and the stack collapses, casting debris and a plume of fire into the small room.

The old man raises the shotgun toward the girl.

Adelaide advances quickly, thrusting the knife forward, and into his chest.

She had expected it to be like cutting chicken, or an apple. Smooth and exacting. Little resistance. She had imagined the knife would slide right through his flesh, and sever his heart, his lungs.

But men are not apples.

The blade lands higher than she had planned, just below his armpit, skipping across bone, snagging skin, and spinning out of her grasp. It tumbles through the air, the descent as idle as the snow falling outside her window.

Adelaide has delivered little more than a scratch.

The old man buckles, hollers, and spins toward her. His knuckles land across her jaw, and Adelaide drops to the floor, the smell of lantern fluid filling her lungs.

The old man points to Adelaide, scolding. "You did this, you god-damned witch."

He aims the shotgun at River's feet.

River holds aloft her log of fire.

The man pulls the trigger.

There is a click.

River jolts as if she has been hit. Adelaide jolts as if she has been hit. But no bullets were fired. Only a click.

He tries again.

Click.

Adelaide sees the barrel now. It is dented, bent, the buckshot unchambered. Outside, Brother #1 had smashed it against the ground, the trees. So much rage. So much madness.

The old man freezes, appraising his damaged weapon, as River launches her burning log.

It hits the old man's shoulder and rolls away—across the living room, past the sofa, and into the wreckage of the broken side table.

The puddle of lantern fluid erupts into flame.

Adelaide stares at the small blaze in her cabin and looks to River. The girl wears an expression that Adelaide has seen once before—when River braved the mirror for the first time. An expression of nonbelief, of not trusting her own eyes. Adelaide understands that feeling—she's known it well these last few weeks.

The fire grows quickly, feeding, burgeoning, and River screams as somewhere outside, the wild woman howls.

The dogs yelp and bark, maddened by the sound, and Adelaide runs to River, scooping the girl into her arms as the old man stands tall, surrounded by flames.

He lumbers about her cabin, growing, growing, as the fire rages. His skin is maroon and black against the brilliance of it.

The flames spill into her kitchen, pool against her cupboards. A cloud hovers in her home like a swarm of locusts, and it, too, is growing, growing.

Hounds wail at her front door.

The smoke clogs Adelaide's lungs, and she presses River's face to her chest to protect her. They must escape. Together. The bedroom window has offered release once tonight. It will do so again.

Adelaide takes a step toward the bedroom.

"Go on now," the old man says. "Go on and see what's waitin' for ya."

Adelaide wishes she could carry River far from this place. Her face is bruised, her ribs likely broken, her shins are bleeding, and there's a gaping hole in her thigh leaving dark puddles in her wake. She has denied the pain in her body for too long and can fight it no more.

But the bedroom door is right there. *Right there!*

"I told you, I ain't leavin' till I get what I came for, animal bitch or not," the old man says. "You've made it difficult, but I'll make it real easy for you. Your choice, I s'pose." He spits on her floor.

The old man grasps the sofa and thrusts it toward Adelaide and River. Just a little.

A warning.

Adelaide places her foot on the sofa and shoves it away. It sails to the other side of the living room. Beneath the floorboard that pulls away from the nails, the chain jangles. A warning of her own.

Yes-yes-yes.

Adelaide drops River to the floor and throws herself atop the floor-board, prying up the board and gathering the heavy chain into her arms. The teeth. The jaws. The trap.

The old man lunges forward. "Oh no, you—"

But Adelaide is practically a professional now, and she has the trap set before the old man can take another step. She thrusts it at him, and he backs away, hands in the air.

The smoke grows thicker in the cabin. River coughs, and throws her hands around Adelaide's leg, burying her face in her skirt.

This is over now. It is time to go.

With the trap held out before her, Adelaide shuffles backward, pulling the child into her bedroom and toward the window promising oxygen and freedom.

Something collapses in her kitchen, and sparks erupt into the living room.

The old man watches as Adelaide and River collapse against the bedroom window. He doesn't approach.

Maybe he's letting them go.

The old man whistles and her bedroom is suddenly engulfed by the sound of barking dogs. The hounds are right outside the bedroom window now, blocking their exit, and Adelaide understands why the man wasn't concerned with their retreat.

The flames lick the door frame of the bedroom.

From the living room, his voice. "You can come on out here, right now. Hand that girl over, and you can leave through the front door, while you still have one. I'll leave you be, you have my word. Or you can both burn alive in that bedroom."

The hounds are thunderous behind them. The fire is hot before them.

"My dogs ain't so reasonable. Best decide quick."

Adelaide grips the trap tighter.

She looks down at River, and in her eyes she sees a child who believes she is about to die. Adelaide wants to save her from this feeling. A child should never believe such things. But here they sit, beneath a window that offers no escape, surrounded by fire consuming inch by inch of her sanctuary, the air becoming thicker with every billow of smoke.

Adelaide feels it, too—the inescapability of death. But she cannot give into it. She clashes against it, refuses to accept it. Because once she believes it—once she *truly* believes it—she will stop fighting, too.

The front door is wide open, barren.

The fire in Adelaide's living room grows larger, and she can no longer see the old man. But he must be *somewhere*.

Adelaide stands. The trap in her hand has grown so heavy, weighing a hundred pounds—now a thousand—and she struggles to hold it upright. But this may be their only chance, and she must take it before the flames consume her cabin completely.

She stumbles toward the bedroom door, halting when she spots the old man by the fireplace.

He whistles, and a fury of hounds surge from the back of her cabin to the front, raging anew through the opening of the front door.

The old man points to Adelaide and whistles once more. The dogs test the front steps but do not enter. They jump up and down, strings of saliva flashing like falling stars in the light of the fireplace. The man bellows at them and points again, but the dogs cannot take their eyes off the flames. Away from River. And they refuse to enter the burning cabin.

The old man's face transforms into something brutal and tyrannous.

Adelaide retreats from the doorway, but he approaches quickly, closing the gap between them. The trap trembles in her hand, its teeth sharp and ready.

The trap wants to close. It wants to snap shut, destroy, kill.

Get off my property! Get off my goddamned property!

She cannot allow him to enter. He cannot come in. He cannot be inside her bedroom. Not again.

Adelaide loosens her grip on River. The girl clamors to stay attached, but Adelaide pushes her back, against the window.

Adelaide holds the trap above her head like a hammer. Like an axe. The old man stands outside the fire. His face glows, bright yellow flames dancing in the pools of his eyes.

If Adelaide waits any longer, he will enter her bedroom. Her aim would be better if she allowed him closer, but she cannot risk it. Surely she has earned a small triumph after all she's been through, all she's lost.

Just one accurate throw.

Adelaide aims for his face, his neck, but as soon as the trap leaves her grasp, she knows she's made a mistake. She had not considered the heavy chain, dangling down and snaking across her floor. The resistance of it overpowers her, and the trap, once aloft and determined, now falters. Adelaide shuts her eyes. She cannot watch.

The old man screams, and tumbles back into the living room, landing hard against the floor, yelping at the trap latched to his pant leg. He is hit, but the metal jaws don't clamp through bone and muscle—only skin and fabric.

Adelaide rushes to River, trembling beneath the window.

"Stand up!" Adelaide screams at River, and the girl obeys as if these are words she has practiced.

Something bangs against the bedroom window and Adelaide jumps. Teeth and eyes, tongues and claws. The dogs snarl, blanketing the glass with foam.

The flames breach the bedroom.

Adelaide is tall enough to jump over them, but River is not. Just past the wall of flame, the front door gapes open, offering reprieve in the cool, dark air beyond.

Adelaide watches the old man wrestle the trap from his pant leg. He hollers, but Adelaide cannot hear his words over the roar of the fire.

The room grows hotter, the air dense. Adelaide coughs. River coughs. Time is running out.

Adelaide dives for her closet, grabbing everything large, everything thick. Dresses, coats, bedsheets. Her body collapses under the weight of it all, too injured and exhausted to retrieve any more.

She cloaks River in all of it. Adelaide ties something around the girl's head, bundling it beneath her neck. She wraps something else around her shoulders, tying the ends into a knot at the girl's throat. It may be a bedsheet or it may be a dress. Adelaide does not know. She has stopped recognizing anything as her own. Nothing matters but River. Only River.

Behind their heads, the bedroom window explodes, and the end of the chain strikes Adelaide as the trap crashes through the glass. She clutches her jaw as the hounds erupt with renewed fury, scratching and digging at the splintering window frame.

And then the old man steps toward the threshold, over the fire, and into Adelaide's bedroom.

It has happened once again.

His pant leg is torn, and blood courses freely from a gash on his shin. His eyes rage alongside the flames, and he is no longer a father, a grandfather, a farmer, a hunter. Not old or frail or consumed with sorrow. Adelaide had been hoping for mercy, awaiting a shred of benevolence. But beyond that familiar, dark bewitchment, his eyes are empty. The old man is truly the monster that has lived in her mind all the years, and nothing more.

He snatches Adelaide's ankle, and she kicks him away, pushing herself farther against the wall. He draws closer, reaches for her again.

The old man spits through his teeth. "I ain't tryin' to hurt you, witch."

A dark shape leaps over Adelaide—a petite figure draped in coats and bedsheets.

River chirps into the air, frightened sounds, panicked sounds, as she waddles closer to the fire, toward the living room and the open door beyond.

The old man moves toward River, and Adelaide throws herself forward, but pain cripples her, bends her in half, and she can only watch as River toddles closer to the fire.

Escaping.

Leaving Adelaide behind.

River dashes through the flames, a tail of fabric sparking in her wake.

She stands in the living room, screeching sounds into the night—sounds like breaking china, like screeching lambs, and Adelaide wants to say, Stop, don't go, wait for me. But the girl does not look back.

Adelaide doesn't realize the dogs have left her bedroom window until she sees them beyond her front door once again. They whine, growl, as a girl bundled in smoking fabric draws closer.

River stops in the living room and howls through the open door. Somewhere outside, the wild woman howls. The dogs whimper and circle one another in the doorway.

Adelaide needs to run. She needs to snatch the girl and leave this place, together. Always together. But first, she must stand.

It is a challenge, and her limbs are slow to submit.

River does not see the old man step over the flames and reach for her, but Adelaide does. She tries to scream but her throat is clogged with smoke, and she crawls forward, retching against the floor.

The old man's arms are crooked and outstretched, his body misshapen and disfigured in the light. By time. Isolation. Some people shouldn't live in the woods, secluded from the rest of the world. Some people become indulgent and self-important. Or they become something else altogether.

The old man grabs the girl, and the dogs whoop.

River wails.

The wild woman wails.

Adelaide wails.

The old man lifts the child from the floor, and she kicks the air, her legs landing on nothing.

Adelaide lunges toward the bedroom door but the flames are higher now, and the heat singes her skin, her eyebrows. Behind her, a shard of glass falls from the frame, detonating against the floor. The dogs leave their post at the front door to circle back to her bedroom window, hungry for the source of the sound.

River sinks her teeth into the old man's hand, and he screams, dropping the girl and cradling his wrist.

River rolls across the floor, tangled in fabric still smoking at the ends. She slips from the mass of clothes and bedsheets to stand naked in the living room. She looks back at Adelaide and pauses, mouth stained red, an arc of flame traveling the wall behind her.

The front door gapes open, abandoned and offering release, but River waits for her.

She waits for her.

Adelaide considers wrapping a blanket around herself as well, but there is no more time. There is never enough time. The clock in her bedroom ticks away, scorning every second she's already lost. It mocks her now, more than ever. *Tick-tick-tick.* She hears the old man's voice in the sound. The voices of his sons.

Witch-witch-witch.

Adelaide leaps through the bedroom doorway. Her skirt billows through the flames, just as River's had, but instead of singeing the edges, Adelaide's skirt erupts into an inferno as the fire ignites the lantern fluid soaked through the fabric.

Adelaide stumbles, collapsing on top of the old man, her weight forcing him to the floor. His head hits the wood and he spits a tooth from his mouth.

His expression is one of rage as he stares at Adelaide atop him.

And then it is a look of panic as he begins to burn.

Adelaide and the old man—burning, screaming, smoke spiraling and sheeting against their bodies.

River—flailing, shouting something. *Something.*

Three dogs at the bedroom window—howling through broken glass, bloody noses, crazed eyes.

Something snaps high above, like a tree branch. Or the beam of a cabin roof.

All around her, the smell of burning hair, burning skin, burning muscle.

Outside, a wild woman—running, moaning.

Inside, a witch—cursing, clinging.

And a child—wanting to run and stay, all at the same time, torn between her two mothers.

Adelaide cannot go with River. She knows this now.

Somewhere outside is a basket with clothing that will never be worn and food that will never be eaten. There is a butter-yellow knitted cap that will sink into the forest floor with the next snowfall. And a piece of paper bearing the name of a woman who will never know she nearly found an old lady and a little girl on her doorstep this night. If only they'd left sooner. If only they'd been faster.

The old man is still strong after all these years, but Adelaide is stronger. Perhaps it is her anger that gives her an edge. Perhaps it is River. Adelaide is younger than the man, and taller. It did not help her all those years ago, but her legs wrap around him now with ease, even as he beats his fists upon her back.

The flames engulf her legs, sparking against his pants, and he screams as Adelaide fastens her body against his, inching him toward her bedroom window, farthest from the front door. Farthest from River.

To a place where the dogs can see.

28

Adelaide pulls the old man through the wall of flame and into her bedroom.

He struggles, clawing at her back, his neck twisting from side to side. He juts his head forward but does not make contact, and Adelaide buries her head into his neck as he labors beneath her.

The dogs wail at the bedroom window, unable or unwilling to brave the broken glass and enter her burning cabin, as she tightens her embrace around their master.

The old man releases a sound that bubbles from his mouth, as though he is underwater.

It is not that Adelaide doesn't feel the pain of the fire—it is the worst pain she's felt in all her life, like her skin is splitting and peeling away from the muscle. Maybe it is. She wants to run from this kind of pain, scream through it, feel hate and anger at it. Even so, the burning of her flesh is nothing compared to the torment of being pressed against the old man. But every lick of fire that pops against her skin burns him as well, and she embraces him tighter.

This man who entered her home in the middle of the night (eyes frenzied and aglow, ripping her clothes, pinning her down) is beneath her very body right now, ablaze.

She hopes he feels helpless and violated. She hopes he wants to vomit. She hopes he feels alone. She hopes he wants to die.

She'd told him to stay off her goddamned property, but he didn't listen. *He didn't listen.*

The old man gags, the sound so close to her ear that she feels the wetness of it against her face. He kicks the wall, and the clock tumbles from its nail, whispering a simple *tick-tick-tick* before exploding against the floor.

Adelaide looks past the flames, and locks eyes with River.

The girl stands bare as a wild animal amid a ring of fire, the light glistening off her damp skin like moonlight on the water, Adelaide's secret spot. The girl's hair is untamed like the ferns that grow below the canopies in the spring.

Adelaide wishes she could say something to the girl, but she has so few words left, and River wouldn't understand them anyway. So Adelaide smiles, and hopes that is enough because it is all the two of them have left to share.

In the kitchen, the ceiling collapses. River flinches but does not move. Adelaide wants to scream at her to go, but the smoke has rendered her throat useless.

The living room window implodes, showering the girl with glass. Still, she does not move. River watches, captivated, her arms limp on either side of her torso.

The fire is at Adelaide's throat now. Her sleeves are aflame, and her eyes burn. She squeezes them shut. When she opens them again, everything has clouded over. But she can still see River.

And something else.

Something galloping on all fours.

A wild mane of black matted curls—the wild woman scooping up her daughter, carrying River out of the cabin and into the night.

Adelaide wants that to be the last thing she sees, so she closes her eyes.

Beneath her, the old man has gone silent. He no longer moves. Adelaide clings tighter to him still, and smells her hair burning. She exhales the stench, unsure if she will draw another breath.

She will not.

Her chest closes, and her throat closes, and her mouth closes, and Adelaide is no longer there at all. Not really. Adelaide is in the river now, where the water forms a symphonic eddy, and red leaves drift somewhere high above her. The water is warm.

It is magnificent.

❀

The girl stands with mother beneath brother's favorite tree—the one that has the curly flowers now that the pale rain is gone, and together, they watch the place where the cabin once stood.

The girl looks to the trees, which are now the color of the sky at night, and she looks to the garden, where brother still sleeps in the dirt. And she thinks of the woman who loved her like a mother, and knows that the woman isn't hurt anymore.

When the girl was in the cabin, she felt when the woman's hurt went away. It was when the woman glowed like the sun, like a piece of tree from the fireplace. When she hugged the man, down on the ground, and he became like a piece of tree from the fireplace, too. That's when the woman's hurt went away.

Mother leans down and pushes her forehead against the girl's forehead, and River pushes back.

River is hungry. She hopes mother takes her to find the plants with the curly green leaves that stick out from beneath the ground. Or the fat, creamy roots shaped like fingers that are buried under the plant that no longer has the fuzzy flowers. Because even though the pale rain has passed, it is still very cold, and they must dig and hunt every day, otherwise they will not eat for many days and many nights. And then they'll be buried in the square forest like brother.

Something dashes across their path and mother nearly attacks, but the girl holds her back.

It's not food, the girl says.

Mother says, Yes, it is.

Trust me, the girl says.

And mother does.

The two of them stand quietly and watch the chicken hunt for bugs beneath leaves and in between rocks.

This is the woman's chicken. The girl can say *chic-ken* now, and she does, and mother beams and smiles at the strange word. They watch the bird scurry this way and that, excited by everything he sees. And then he dashes away, disappearing beyond the trees.

The girl squeezes mother's hand and asks, Can we come back here again?

And mother says, Perhaps another day.

She has told her mother about her new name, and she hopes mother can learn to say it. She will tell mother about brother's new name, too.

Perhaps another day.

She practices her name as they walk.

"Ri-ver."

"Ri-ver."

"River."

The girl smiles at mother, and mother smiles back.

Above them is the bird that makes the *yeep* sound.

❀

Acknowledgements

To my earliest readers—my mother, father, Jen van Kaam, Annike Karlson, and Thomas Halvorsen. Your support gave me the confidence to continue on this path, and there aren't enough words to express my thanks.

To my agent, Nicki Richesin. Thank you for loving *Thieves, Beasts & Men* as much as I do, and for seeing through my intense over-writing to the heart beating beneath. I look forward to working with you on every future project!

To my editor, Lilly Golden. I felt as though my opinions were highly respected throughout the entire process, and I couldn't be more grateful! Thank you for being a champion of my art and encouraging it to be a part of this book.

A huge thank you to my cover designer, Erin Seaward-Hiatt, for turning my photography into a stunning cover worthy of praise. And to my publicist, Sophie James, for all the incredible efforts you've made on behalf of Adelaide and her wild family. My copyeditor, Susan Barnett, proofreader, Diane Wood, and *everyone* at Arcade, Skyhorse, and Wendy Sherman Associates, Inc.

To Dean Tsoupeis, whose daughters served as models for two of the illustrations in this book. I hope I honored them well.

To Gabriel Cole, and all our date-night-read-aloud sessions by candlelight. Your excitement over Adelaide, River, Little Bird, and the wild woman made me fall in love with this book all over again, as though reading it for the very first time.

To my amazing kid who was witness to every step. The struggles, the tears (breakdowns), and all the little celebrations along the way. I made sure you saw it all so you'd know that the only failure in chasing your dream is to stop chasing. I recognize and appreciate the amazing human you already are and can't wait to see what you do next. I'm your biggest fan.

And to my readers. The act of writing a book is the act of taking a small piece of who you are and crafting an entire world around it. I *was* Adelaide for the year it took to write the first draft, and as I sit here now, part of me still lounges in that river under the maple tree. Still lights the fireplace. Still tends to a garden that once had a gate.

Reading a book is one of the most intimate of acts, and I thank you for taking a peek. I hope you enjoyed spending time in Adelaide's world as much as I enjoyed creating it.

About the Author

Shan Leah is an award-winning fine artist, freelance photographer, and lover/writer of dark literary fiction. Surrounded by an endless supply of pens, papers, paints, and clay, Shan grew up in the Florida Keys and was taught proper wheel-throwing techniques before mastering her shoe laces. She currently lives in St. Petersburg, Florida, with her brilliant son and small herd of cats. She finds beauty dreadfully boring.

Reader's Guide Questions

1. How does the setting of the novel support the story?
2. How do you feel about the decisions Adelaide made throughout the book? To trap the beast? To keep the children? To burn the farm?
3. Regardless of Adelaide's motives, following the thread of the narrative, did Adelaide's actions ultimately result in endangering the wild family or saving them?
4. How does the title relate to the book, and how does it change as the story unfolds? Who are the thieves in this novel? Who are the beasts?
5. Should the wild woman have been aggressive in trying to retrieve her children? Why do you think she took a more passive role?
6. How does Adelaide's suicide attempt at the beginning influence the ending?
7. There are two dueling elements in *Thieves, Beasts & Men*: water and fire. How do these opposing forces play into the story?
8. Would you consider this a tragic ending? Or a happy one?

9. The author gives us very little backstory for each of the characters. Why do you think that is?

10. Tales of the unreliable narrator are often the most intriguing kind. Why do you think they're so appealing? Does *Thieves, Beasts & Men* fit into this category?

11. What was your initial reaction when you first met Adelaide's daughter? Mother-daughter relationships can be fraught under the best of circumstances. Imagine now, growing up in total isolation with your mother. How does Adelaide's relationship with her daughter differ from that of the wild woman's and River?

12. How do you think River's experience living with Adelaide might impact her future in the wild? How has she been irrevocably altered by the acquisition of Adelaide's language? How does language shape our lives?

13. Sexual assault leaves lasting wounds. Why do you think Adelaide chose to stay in her cabin all these years despite the continued threat of the old man?

14. Why do you think people are so drawn to the idea of removing themselves from society and becoming self-sufficient? Have you ever considered leaving mainstream life behind to live a solitary life in the woods?

15. How does the inclusion of the author's artwork impact your experience as a reader?

16. Tales of feral people have been popular for ages, dating back at least as far as Edgar Rice Burroughs' 1912 novel *Tarzan of the Apes*. Why do you think this is such an alluring topic? How do the trappings of civilization alter the core human mind and experience?

17. One of the most remarkable biographical elements about the author is that she dropped out of high school after tenth grade. How does knowing this impact your own impression of formal secondary and post-secondary education? Can formal education stifle an artistic mind or expand it?